Y0-BVP-687

The Drinking of Spirits

stories by

Tom Abrams

Livingston Press
at
The University of West Alabama

ISBN 0-942979-69-9, cloth
ISBN 0-942979-70-2, paper

Library of Congress Card Number: 00-102607

Printed in The United States of America.

Cloth binding: Heckman Bindery
Printing:

Cover photos: Tricia Taylor
Text layout and design: Joe Taylor
Proofreading: Charlie Loveless, Kim Smith,
Kathleen Parnell, Mary Pagliero

The Drinking of Spirits

For Jane

The Parade

My girlfriend has told me for a year now, whenever I go someplace without her, "Don't bring anything home with you." I never knew quite what that meant, until the other day when I went to the Gasparilla parade. I don't guess I ever wondered what they did with a parade once it reached its destination. I never was at the end of a parade, always somewhere in the middle. But far as I can tell now, what they do is pick out one of the viewers, I really have no idea what qualities you must possess to be considered, and that person gets to take the parade home with him. I suspect that children are usually the recipients of the parade. How the mistake was made I don't know, but the parade is now at my house, and how long it's going to stay is still up in the air.

I first noticed it early the next morning. The sun hadn't gotten up yet, but I could see that my bedroom wasn't right. Not that it had changed physically, but by the fact that there were a great many people passing through. I suspected that I was dreaming. But when the people stood still momentarily, my bed began to move and everyone was cheering so that I must confess I got caught up in it and waved once or twice to the crowd. It never dawned on me to perhaps check the side of the bed to see whom I was representing. This was, I'm afraid, a vital loss of information. I mean I'm still pretty much in the dark here.

The last few days it's toned down some, become more subtle, moved into the corner of my eye, plays hide and seek really. Possibly, I think, because I pointed it out to my girlfriend. It never occurred to me before that such a public spectacle as a parade would have a private side. Or that something so large could act so small over what my girlfriend said. "I don't want it in the house," is how she put it. She didn't mind at first, but when the parade stayed on, and she'd had her fill of cotton candy and Sno-kones, she changed her tune. What bothers me is that she somehow blames me for it being here.

I've tried taking photographs of the parade, perhaps as proof that it really is in my home. Maybe to show them to my friends. I haven't invited any of my friends over lately; it's so crowded here. But the photos never come out just right, no matter how careful I am. They're somehow odd, as if the human beings are there by accident, and they're standing vaguely off to the side, or in a corner, and always out of focus, as if really what I meant to take was a picture of the wall. Or perhaps it is like the camera took the picture by itself, and for itself, and its concerns were not for the people in the parade, but maybe for the way the light was.

This isn't something I would take to the law, even if I had proof. For that matter, there's a policeman right across the way. He seems to be having a pleasant time. It wouldn't be right to change his mood. It's not every day you see one smiling on the job. There are some deplorable scenes he could deal with I guess. For example, there has been an old lady asleep on the porch for several hours. She really is old. She could be my grandmother, the way she has her nylons rolled down below her knees. I refuse to believe that she is drunk.

And even if she is, well then, God bless her. Because to tell you the truth, I've really begun to enjoy this, all of it. Though I swear, I cannot meet the mayor of our town even one more time. How could he not remember me? It is a small house that we live in. And I like it more because I fear it just won't last. You cannot forever have that cool wind off Bayshore roaming in your bedroom. And there is a certain laziness creeping in, like when one thing is over and another is about to begin. The crowd seems to be breaking up. The faces look a little too serious and some people are obviously lost. And there has been some chaos this past day, as there was near the end of the parade when people walked among the bands.

But maybe it will all come back around. And if I see myself there among the crowd, or some of my friends, I might get an explanation. There is only one thing I can remember that seemed out of the way. I heard a voice that day call my name. But no, when I looked around, there was no one. I remember thinking, it must have been someone from another day. For I have seen many parades. But I bet they were calling out my name just then because this one was mine. At any rate, I think I'll enjoy it as long as I can. It's too good to last, I know. It's the kind of thing people tend to kill after awhile, even though they don't mean to. Yes, I think I'll just go get a hotdog with mustard, see what comes along next.

Small Arms Fire

In front of you dolphins muscle up from the sea. The water is wrinkled and full of green ribbons. The bottle beside you is a dead soldier. In a burst, the bird with the other world concealed under its wing explodes into flight. You wince, and then let it go. A smile just starts in the corners of your mouth; it never gets anywhere.

To the left the shore turns, angles out like a long white road, peppered by tanks, APC's, trucks, tents, men in fatigues. Because of them, you can sit here with your back against the war.

Heat bends the air. Human motion has moved to blue—the heads on the water, the bodies cut at the waist, the knee. The bolts of color are the daughters and small sons of the women hired to fill sandbags for the airstrip at Quang Tri. You see but cannot hear them. The wind takes their voices inland.

There's a girl in an orange blouse. She's wading toward you, watching her feet. Now, chasing minnows, she misses, kicks water into the air. Each drop falls down with a sun in it.

You look at her awhile, her narrow hips thrust sideways as she stands at rest. A child will ride there sometime not far perhaps. By the age of twenty she will be old. But at the moment she is young and uncommonly pretty. More daughters take shape. The world starts, and your sight spreads out; she disappears into it.

Rafael is walking along the shore. He strolls over like a young prince at the end of his journey. He's from the South. His voice is full of black cotton.

"Where you goin'?"

"Nowhere," he says. "You want to come along?"

"C'mere."

He sits down, hands you a j.

"How'd it go?"

"The truck's where it was. . . . We couldn't get it any closer." He wipes his nose on his wrist. "Mumaw's guardin' it. Want a keep him out my eyes long as I can."

"Billy get ice?"

"I don't know. . . . He was last seen lookin' in the truck mirror, tryin' to figure out if he was still present I guess. A big piece of information missin' there, even for a cook. The boy took one too many headers. Used to know where Spaceman was. He was taggin' me around, but I lost'm. . . . You notice his tattoo? Say he got it on R&R. A tattoo of Elmer Fudd. How fucked up at the time are you to get a tattoo of Elmer Fudd put on your arm? Buchanan . . . I jus' saw him a minute ago. What's that other one's name . . . the one got ringworm?"

They had real names, but their war names were closer to the truth: Gila, June-bug, 8-Ball, Fish. . . .

"Fish. Yeah. He's out lookin' for a small wound. Who'd I miss?"

"Guy-jacks."

Rankled, he says, "He's the last word, ain't he?"

"I thought he was your buddy."

"He saved my death. What do I owe him? Fire that up, Doc."

His eyes inhale the scene.

"Ain't it rare?"

He picks up the bottle, holding it to the sun at arm's length.

"A fifth of Eden . . . mmm . . . purple Jesus." He takes the last nip, shuddering. The skin makes x's on the back of his neck.

"Damn, that is *rough.* You drank all that?"

"I drank part of it. After which, I spilled most of it. Then I drank what there was."

"Just as well. . . . Whyn't you in swimmin'?"

"I don't know how."

His eyes fix on you. "You got 37 days and a wake-up. You startin' to miss this place already?

"I locked up your piece," he went on. "It weighs the same as mine I notice. It's not like you said."

Your rifle had grown so strangely heavy of late, you could barely lift it.

"Hey, you gotta hear this joke. . . ."

"O" you say, for your thoughts are now traveling in circles of smoke.

Part of the morning goes by you and down the road into the past. You're looking at Rafael, his nose hooked, too far from his face. His skin is coal-blue. Hawklong, his stare is a cage he has closed on the scene. All around him the air is blonde.

He says, "I was thinkin' 'bout Spaceman."

"Thinkin' what?"

"I wonderin' what in the world his parents are like. . . ."

After awhile you say, "Rafael . . . you findin' what you need?"

"It ain't far, I reckon. It's always jus' yonder. I'll be alright. I go home . . . I'll drink my Seagram Gin, drink my Log Cabin . . . shit jus' get me by is all."

"You ought to kick."

"You ought a jus' leave me alone on it. You always harpin' . . . goddamn it." The sun is so sharp it cuts his eyes to the ground. "You 'n everyone."

"Just the same . . . seems like it's gainin' on you."

"No matter where I run to, I meet myself there . . . no way around that. But what's it matter? I kill myself, or I keep on dyin'. . . . Shit jus' take the edge off my thinkin' on it."

Rafael stands. Wearing the clouds like scarves on his shoulders, he grins; then the sand steps him away. His body cuts a black path through noon.

Your skin is right up against the sun. Soon, sleep burns through time.

Then, and it seemed only a moment that you were away, from the place where you have lain down in your life, you rise, and wake—to the electrical whine of gulls. The world looks back at you, a strange creature in a field of objects. The dream you were having goes away without saying goodbye. But a character is left behind, something like a man, brick-red in color, a long goat face, eye-sockets of white heat. The description of a devil, perhaps, yet it does not seem to be this. The expression on its face is really sort of kind. Out of its element, it stumbles about, dissolves. You don't even recall it after its gone.

You're smoking a menthol. Your eyes catch on aspects of your appearance. Salt has formed white lines that jag through the dirt in your fatigues. Your boots are dull red from mud. A tan circles your shoulders and stops, where the flak jacket you always wear ends.

Some kids find you. A half dozen of them. They're selling beer, the cans covered with cold sweat. Then she comes again; the world falls away behind her step. She stops, looks at you and smiles, then starts again. Her hair flows behind her like black wind. Her complexion is bamboo. She's wearing that orange blouse, black pajama bottoms. Her feet are bare and callused. Close by now, she smells of the sea. The shadow of a companion cuts her face in half vertically: one eye is coal, the other diamond.

You try to speak, but the words are swollen with both death and hunger. Your teeth feel like corn.

She tells you her name is Lee. When you tell her yours, she's amused. Out of nervousness, you have spoken your full name. Even you have not heard it for a long time.

"Where does this long name come from?" she asks.

"It's Hungarian."

"I have never heard of this place," she says. "How may I call you?"

"They call me Doc."

She says, "I am part French."

The wind tilts, and the other kids come back into their places. They bring out their wares. Lee takes an opium ball from a young girl beside her and kneads it into the shape of a flower. She holds it up saying, "The hand of an angel."

When they see how fat your wallet is, a covey of voices takes to the air.

"Souvenir?" Lee says. But her smile reaches into irony. It's an easy smile and shorn of all malice.

They want to exchange money. Their piasters for your scrip, which they call dollars. A girl attempts to explain the transaction.

"See . . . souvenir . . . twentee dolla' 'merican, you twentee piaster. Changee." She moves her hands to show you how it goes.

"Never happen," you say.

"Pot, too," a boy says. He takes a cellophaned ten-pack from his hat. You shake your head. He takes out another, and then a third. They like to bargain. It's a kids' game to them. Sometimes they get carried away. And you're just playing, too. The money means nothing to you. You have a lot of it. In the mountains there's nothing to buy with it.

"Thirty beaucoup," Lee says.

"And beer," you say.

"Neva hack it, g.i.," a tough kid says.

Lee takes a can of beer, opens it.

"We will trade now . . . okay? Please." And she smiles again, and it touches you in that place the flowers are in winter.

She leaves, comes back, leaves and returns on her journey through the hour. Now and again, she helps her mamasan, takes money to her, something. Her mother looks unbearably old. She is dry leather in clothes, a black smile. Her once distinguished features have been completely folded away.

You go off by yourself, not knowing what to think. For a man can be a magician but then he comes upon desire. The wind seems to blow the world out.

June-bug shuffles by. He sees you and you see him and maybe you nod to each other, or maybe you just think you did.

June-bug hadn't ever been such a bright light, but he wasn't always blanked out like now. One night on guard duty, he'd left his bunker to take a leak and got lost on the perimeter. He cleared the mine field without a scratch and somehow always taking the wrong turn ended up in the jungle for a week. He'd come to a small clearing and found two heads stuck on poles out there. He knew one of the men. They had been friends. What he couldn't get out of his mind was that they had grown beards after they were dead. Now he shuffled around like an old man with the eyes of a saint, and he wasn't nineteen yet.

Lee comes to you, puts her ear to your shoulder.

"You disappeared . . . I turned around, and you were gone."

The sun is knocking on the water. There is one gull in the hang of the wind. And she only takes your hand into hers, but she has touched you deeper than you can follow.

"You must look at me first," she says.

"What?"

"You must look at me," she says.

The two of you are walking down the shore. There must be some place here to call your own. You come to where a tank is set up, aimed at the day. You catch the radioman's voice in passing. He shoots the breeze. A young girl appears from behind the tank. She isn't wearing much, and her smile is a hook. When she is past, Lee calls her *the girl with three mouths.*

Farther on, there is another girl with soldiers around her. They are not hidden well. These are ARVN troops. Useless, to your way of thinking. A month ago, at a camp named C-2, some ARVN had fired on the kids scavenging a trashpile, killing three of them.

Lee says, "He numba ten."

You look back roughly with your eyes. This time you see it is a young boy. Caught in fantasy, he wears a rope leash at his neck. His face is a mask of lipstick and rouge, smeared absurdly. It's difficult to believe the lines that have eaten into your face in less than a year, but here they are again, dining on a frown.

Then she repeats it: "You must look at me."

She takes you into a grove of palms, into the shade and the penciled light; you walk through design. She sits down in a shadow that trembles about her like dark mercury. Lifting her blouse, she shows you a secret that her clothes have kept. Her nipples are obliterated. She is marked by the fairest scars, like intricate webs, though their beauty is separate from loveliness. You begin to say something, but her face is turned away.

Red earth skeins the sand here like the roads on a map. In the distance behind you, the blue-green mountains roll up into a frozen sea, its waves caught in arced stillness. Each horizon is a bridge across the river of color. The tide has a voice, and the wind answers it. There is a radiance of pale sulfur below the palms, grape shadow, lilac. And her at your side as if you had been divided in two.

She is asleep. Her eyes move rapidly under their lids, trying to keep up with her dream. The two of you made love and then fell asleep, and you woke soon after like an animal you felt so innocent. These are the first hours you have been friends with yourself . . . for how long? You've been alone, lost with the holes in your days; and now, as though a photograph had been taken that froze you in this moment, she frames your shoulder.

You think, She is a woman; she has never been a child; there's no time for that in this country.

And you have to smile, recalling the reason you're here—the strange order that came down from Battalion saying that anyone who managed to stay alive for a year would receive an award. Didn't say it that way exactly; it came dressed carefully in military lore. But that was the gist of it. And if any such qualified troop did not deserve an award, the colonel wanted to know, in writing, why not. It was easier to do it than it was not to, in other words, and now you and Rafael are carrying a load of clowns forty miles to service battery so the colonel can pin a decoration on them. The colonel had quit alcohol when he arrived in-country. And he came across as just that, a man badly in need of a drink. You recall the XO as he explained the detail, weighing his words as though they actually had value. There hadn't been much to smile about lately, but it was hard not to just then. Even the guns that night seemed to be laughing.

Top had picked you for the detail to get you off the hill before you totalled, as lately you had gone remote, even your own body only a scene that you are watching from a little way off.

"Pretend it's TDY."

"I need a shotgun."

"Well, I can guess who you want. Sure. Why not? You can leave him there far as I'm concerned."

You smile now, but even if she were awake, she wouldn't have caught it; your mouth doesn't move.

A cloud darkens the sun. She is stirring in her sleep. You don't know where to begin, or how to say to her what you must say to someone at last besides yourself—that you are dying of disguise; always meaning one thing, and being something else. That actually, you are two people, with their backs to each other, cambered so that they will never meet. And how can you describe the waiting, the days, pinballing up to their certain level, and back to their lay, and the nights worse. And the war was bad but the quiet times killed you in a different way, because time did not move then. That is all life is to you now, the waiting on life to begin. Or say, this is the way it's had to be, to close your eyes, to keep from looking any more.

For Death lives here. You have seen it. And you are the pattern of the empty spaces it has left. You have seen it stand tall with broad shoulders; you've seen it come begging in the shadows. You have seen the hills laced with artillery patches, the land gone black; you have seen napalm stretch a quick shadow across a race with the stilling of one child; the good body of a woman turn into a zoo of bullets; scars running like concertina wire down an old man's face, as though he wept so hard the tears burned tracks on him; you have seen a friend's smile stop at mid-youth and go out the back of his head, then had him return that night in a dream saying, Death is a place I've been. Like the must in the addict you feel the wait, but how do you say it?

There is a brief shower. For the moments that it endures, you look out through the bars of the rain.

Through a hole in her sleep, she is looking at you. She is slowly rising within herself. In the sequence of a wind, a black snow falls, patterns are printed in air. It is the wind's ink. Time blinks like an owl. An episode from yesterday morning enters. Once again you pass the old peasant crumpled by the side of the road. The mine he detonated had taken off like a terribly quick bird and touched him with its wings. A mongoose gnaws at his armpit; one hand jerks back and forth, as if the dead man were gesturing you to come closer.

Touching your arm, she gives it muscle, nerve. She is holding you. Her hands make you into the shape of a man, as they lead you back to the present.

"I've been alone. I don't know if I can talk to anyone but myself."

She says, "I feel, too."

She moves slightly, and the sun is stranded in her hair.

She says, "When will you return?"

"Tomorrow."

"I will cry."

"I don't understand."

"Tomorrow is too far."

She closes her eyes on your reflection. Your mouths taste bad together, but it doesn't matter. Then the falling, and the earth does not catch you, nor nothing beyond. You are swimming in her now; you have found the door to the sea.

Rafael and you are alone in the tent by the LZ at service battery. He is drifting in and out of his personality. One candle is burning. Outside, a cricket is singing in its best black voice. It's not a cricket like you all are thinking. It sounds like a sawmill in the distance.

"When I die, Doc . . . if you aroun' . . . I want you to set my body afire . . . 'n pour this on it . . . see, here in my boot I keep it. Pour it on the fire, 'n I'll climb the smoke to heaven."

"You're mumbling."

Every shadow has its roots in the light of the candle.

"Each grain is a little map . . . that leads you out of your eyes. . . ." He drifts away, then returns like a stranger to his last thought.

"That Buchanan . . . he's a crazy man. Know what he tell me?—All those I have killed will be my slaves in paradise."

He starts saying it slower now, like the street his thoughts are on is so long, he's not sure they will arrive.

"You gone be leavin' soon, Doc. You gettin' short as hell."

You say nothing.

"Gettin' so short can't hardly see out your eyes no more."

"What's that mean?"

"You always knowed before," he says. He rises, throws the flaps back farther on top of the tent. The wind says something, and the candle weeps. Rafael is a shadow standing in a triangle, the zero moon perched on his shoulder.

"What's bothering you?"

"That gook."

"What about her?"

"None a that shit's any good here."

"What're you talkin' about?"

"Carin'," he says.

Anger comes quick, makes you stumble inside yourself, like a blind boy for the first time out walking his cane.

Rafael turns away, glares at the winking of small arms fire on a distant hill. He was looking into the future, but you didn't understand it just then.

A Tale of Two Losers

Hector Rojo back then was someone who had lost his spark. He'd not called his girlfriend in two months, and she hadn't even bothered to find out why. But here's the reason: About five minutes after their last conversation, she asked a question about the same subject they had just completely exhausted—asked the question like it was a new day or something. "The hell with you," Hector told her. It didn't go over well. Consequently, he hadn't gotten laid since then either. This concerned him. Plus the lotto had failed him of late. That and his girlfriend had been pretty much his sole means of support.

It was Saturday night, and he decided to go down to the Cadillac Lounge, see if he could turn his luck around.

The big lotto prize was seven million dollars that week. Peanuts, to Hector's way of thinking. He liked it better when it was up to 14, 21. There was more adventure at these heights. He had never matched more than three numbers on this, but he was certain it was only a matter of time. He'd already purchased ten tickets. He needed two numbers to finish his eleventh, and he was on the lookout.

The lotto had invested nearly all the commonplace occurrences of Hector's life with the symbolism of figures. House addresses, license plates, picture show stubs, telephone poles, mustaches—anything that could be measured. When he began to play with numbers, suddenly the world contained many worlds. Nothing was any longer irrelevant. The details of each day were now intertwined, had meaning.

In another sense, he had lately begun to regard himself as all but a mathematician. Not that he was so good at multiplication or subtraction or any of that. His skills in this regard were somewhat marginal, but that's beside the point. Here's the point—Hector could begin with virtually any episode in the day and arrive at a corresponding set of numbers.

It was his way of making life accountable. Also, it gave him something to do with his time. He didn't work a regular job, and just after he forgot that he had a girlfriend, his TV broke. There are many more hours in the day when you have no TV, he concluded. About 9. He wrote that down just then.

See him there getting out of the cab? The guy jotting something down on his hand.

Hector wore a long-sleeved yellow shirt tied at the stomach, brown pinstripe trousers rolled up to his ankles, lizard shoes, no socks. Kind of a pork-pie hat, with a long pigtail hanging down his back. This was his notion of style.

Even looking this fine, though, he had difficulty getting past his own doubts. All that symbolism had somewhat clouded his common sense. A guy at the poolhall the previous day had referred to him as "Spranghead." It was said behind his back, but he'd heard it alright.

This night Hector got to drinking rum and orange juice and soon forgot the lotto cutoff. It was well past midnight when the fact caught up with him. Rum and orange juice will do that to you, even though it seems almost a health drink at the time. He took it as another bad turn and felt disgusted with himself. "This is got to change," he said aloud. He was sitting next to his cousin, Malo, at the bar, and his cousin said, "Why?"

Hector looked at him like he was some kind of animal. His cousin said, "What?" Hector got up and walked away. "Same to ya," his cousin said.

That was how it went, and then this old gal with a bulldog mug came and sat down by him at the table he'd taken. It was a table for two, and she pointed this out.

"Yeah? So what," Hector said.

He'd seen her come in earlier. She'd come in with a real looker. A young woman who turned your eye. Hector said at the time, "They bringin' in their moms tonight." But now he corrected himself. She was too ugly to be related to that. She had big, ash-blonde hair that didn't move.

But the waitress came around just then and the lady bought him a drink. So he thought maybe he'd be kind, given the circumstances. These particular circumstances being that he had three dollars and change left.

After the second drink she bought him and he still hadn't spoken, she hazarded a question.

"Do you have a name?" she asked.

Hector looked at her. He was feeling better. He was starting to get out from underneath his own shadow so to speak. Also, it was that time of night the bartenders really start loading up the drinks.

"They call me Redwine," Hector said. This was true. It was his nickname. Nobody called him Hector but himself.

She seemed to study his hair a moment, as if some clue to the name was contained there, but his hair is black so she just went on, like maybe "Redwine" was commonplace in her circles.

"Mr. Redwine," she said, "do you have the time?"

"For what?" It startled him. He just realized maybe she's trying to hit on him or something.

"Well," she said, "I'm hungry." And she flicked her tongue out several times and growled slightly.

It was Australopithecine in origin. Hector was not familiar with protohuman behavior or the words used to describe it. He only knew the hair had suddenly bristled on the back of his neck. But the waitress set down another rum just then, and he felt himself relaxing the grip he had on the chair. She had told the waitress to keep them coming. "When you see his glass is half empty," she'd said, "bring another."

Hector looked around the bar. It was 1:00 Saturday night: *No Man's Land.*

His cousin stumbled by in his sullen way, pointed to Hector's companion, whistled a little under his breath and shook his head. "Rude dog," he commented. It came out pretty loud.

She was not one unaccustomed to disappointment, however, and decided she had not heard that.

But Hector saw that she had, and he was embarrassed by it. His cousin was an asshole. Everyone in the bar knew that, except this lady probably. He heard himself say, "Let's have another," though she herself hadn't drank a thing since she sat down there.

"I dassent," she said. And when she said it that way, like some Deep South belle . . . you know how loneliness speaks a different language than the eye, especially late at night in the Cadillac Lounge. It's so dark in there anyway.

Then out of the blue she sewed it up:

"Ain't that singular," she said and pointed to a guy at a table behind Hector. He was smoking a pipe. The smoke drifting out of the pipe had made what looked to be a perfect number 7. It's sitting on top of the pipe, about a half foot tall. The guy with the pipe is all but unconscious. He don't know nothing.

Hector took out his pad and finished the lotto pick. It sort of overwhelmed him. "I gotta take a leak," he said and went outside.

While he was out there, a couple of the boys had a scuffle in the parking lot. It didn't last long. One fella ran up to the other from the side and caught him flush in the temple with a roundhouse. Nothing broke this guy's fall. He went down like a statue. Hector took the story of it back inside and started telling her about it. Standing up made him realize how drunk he was. And how he felt like talking. He can't hardly keep his mouth shut now, and he's laughing at his own telling of it. You know how alcohol talks funny.

"Yeah," Hector was saying, "he ain't even watching! And all of a sudden he gets *jacked.*"

The word seemed to cause an association in her mind. She put her hand on his leg. Hector started looking at her differently then. He's got that "dassent" in his head. He's thinking, Every word's a toy, is that it?

"Where you from anyway?" he asked.

"Memphis, Tennessee," she said. Her eyes got faraway. "I tell you . . . we had some colorful times down there."

Hector's wondering, What she mean *down there?*

Turns out she's staying with her brother in Tampa for some reason she never says and has taken a job as a cocktail waitress at a bowling alley north of town. She'd put in nine hours of work this day, but somehow came away from it feeling lively.

He's thinking her over. She's a fine woman, came into his mind, but she's so old there's nothin' left. Is she 30 . . . 40? He couldn't tell the difference at the moment.

She moved her hand up.

"Mr. Redwine," she said, "what are you best at?"

"Pardon?"

"We're all good at least one thing. What are you good at?"

Hector thought awhile.

"I can find bird nests pretty good," he said finally.

Mr. Redwine, he's thinking. There's something in repeating a man's name back to him like that. Just something about it. He lit a cigarette, cupped his hands as though guarding the match against a howling wind. He's rolling now. He's also seeing double to the point she's sitting there by him like a modern painting. He tried to come up with the name of a modern painter but couldn't quite get a handle on it.

"Sure you won't have another?" he asked.

"No," she said. "It's the reason I got into all the trouble. . . ." She left it at that, her eyes gone away again.

Now one of the bartenders, Glenn, was saying "Last call!" and started bopping the guys on top the head who got their heads on the bar.

Hector's thinking, Man . . . I'm gone have to go through with this, right? He'd take her from the back, he'd already decided that. *No, I like it this way!* It's what he'd tell her. Not that she was likely to argue the point. But face to face was out of the question. Then he'd looked at her and decided, in the shadows anyway, she had a kind of lonesome beauty to her. What don't kill you, fattens, he reminded himself. The old saw didn't seem to fit this occasion particularly, but he let it ride. Need to get her out of here before the lights come on, though. He was going back and forth like that.

He needed another drink. A shooter for the road. Meanwhile there'd been a long silence in the conversation. He studied her again. She seemed to be deeply devoted to her hair. Trying for something:

"Yer hair . . ." came tumbling out. He put his thumb and forefinger together, made a circle, like he was giving her hair the OK.

It was sort of captivating headgear, all teased up like that. The word *meringue* came to mind. It didn't seem to want to have a thing to do with her mug. He thought, What a reputation she must have among the mirrors.

"Thank you, Mr. Redwine," she said. "I'll take that as a compliment."

He raised his hand a little, opened it—as if to say, It's nothing.

Then she paid the bar tab and ordered a bottle of rum to go, so that worked out alright, to Hector's way of thinking.

They were sitting there waiting for the rum (which it turns out they don't have a full bottle, or for some reason say they don't, maybe not feeling up to opening a new case at the moment, so she takes a bottle of gin instead and a couple tonics).

"Who was that woman you come with?" Hector asked.

"That was my sister-in-law. My brother's wife. Though," she looked around, "I'm afraid she's deserted me."

"We can take a cab."

"No. I've got my car. But I'm a little concerned about her. . . ."

Hector'd seen her leave an hour ago on the arm of a pipefitter with a long history of drug abuse.

"I wouldn't worry none," he said.

"Her and my brother, they're having some problems." She looked away. She seemed all but embarrassed for some reason, but Hector wasn't one to pursue such things. She was holding out a cigarette for him to light. He didn't even notice that.

"Too bad she didn't stick around. I'd a liked to get to know her."

"You can't always get what you'd druther, Mr. Redwine," she said.

Hector thought, Buddy, you got that shit right.

Then they were heading north in her car. It was a VW of indeterminate age. They thrashed up the interstate.

"My car's not in the best of shape," she confided.

Hector heard himself saying: "Come nut-cuttin' time, these cars'll still be runnin'. . . ." It was like somebody else in there talking. It didn't even sound like his voice.

Her brother rented a house in Sulphur Springs, a derelict two-story wooden structure not far from the river. There was a Harley on the porch that'd been stacked up pretty bad, parts in the front yard scattered around. Before she opened the gate to the fence, she warned him that her brother kept some geese. Four of them.

"They're like watchdogs," she said.

Just as she said this, one of them screamed. Then the other three started up.

They were big, fat geese. Hector'd never heard a goose scream before. It was odd, other-worldly.

They sat at the kitchen table, and she started fixing bologna sandwiches.

"I don't think I can eat no sandwich right now."

"I'm starving," she said. "You can have yours for breakfast maybe."

Hector splashed some gin into a glass.

"Don't bruise that gin, now," she laughed. "Oh, now this onion's a good one—just full of milk. Do you want mayonnaise?" she asked. "Keeping in mind that mayonnaise can turn on you when you least expect it . . . ."

What the hell's she talkin' about now? Hector wondered. He went to the sink, threw some cold water on his face. Out the window in the backyard, four geese stood up and started muttering. There was a clothesline with sheets on it.

"I didn't know you was allowed to keep livestock in the city," he said.

"My brother don't give a shit about what's allowed and what isn't." She said this so hard, Hector turned to look at her.

She downed her sandwich in four bites, but he had stopped counting awhile back. Then she put some music on. They danced in the kitchen. It was a collection of slow and mournful country songs she'd ordered off the TV. Somewhere in here she'd said into his ear, her voice modulated differently, a kind of hush to it: "This is the deal. I'm three months pregnant with somebody else's baby. You know what I want . . . and after tonight, we just forget it happened."

Hector signed on to that last part right away. He started forgetting just when she stopped talking. He's blocked out the rest of that night.

He woke in the morning to a window loud with sunlight in a little bedroom off the kitchen. He staggered to the window and looked out. The wind was snapping the sheets on the line like a fire crackling.

He sat back down on the bed, elbows on his knees, a hand to each side of his head. He didn't truly understand where he was for a time. He was dehydrated. His throat was sore. His hands were shaking so, they shook a cigarette out of the pack without him even trying. He picked up a bottle of tonic from the floor. Taking some of it, he was unmistakenly drunk again.

I got to put myself together, he thought.

He noticed her wig on the bedpost then. It was quite handsome off by itself. It was a thing meant for royalty or a Hollywood movie star. He turned and looked down at her in the bed, pulled the covers away from her face a little. Her features were eroded by sleep, by the light—maybe it was that her head shined so like a cue ball. At any rate, it was a moment both hysterical and terrifying to him.

Now there is something odd and fascinating about all this, just something about it, as Hector would say, but in the end it is an unaccountable thing, a story without meaning or a moral. Only a tale of two losers who happened to find each other in the Tampa night.

Hector was trying to pretend this wasn't the kind of mistake that could ruin someone's life, but on the way out, he ran into her brother. He sat on the back porch drinking coffee in his leathers. He was another version of her but had a long yellow beard down to his waist.

The brother noted the horror on Hector's face, started laughing. And Hector ran from the house into the bright morning with a stranger bellowing "HAW HAW HAW" and four geese screaming at him.

Monroe Puckett

I went down to Red Fred's Bar the other day for lunch, as is my custom. It is the only watering hole in San Antonio, Florida. San Ann is known for its Rattlesnake Festival, held on the third weekend of October each year, and is not remarkable for anything else in particular, except Red Fred's, perhaps. They've got a good lunch special there, and the place fills up at noon. When the lunch crowd clears out, it's usually just me, Buddy Stortch, PeeWee, the Professor, Junior Pike, Kathy the Barmaid, my cousin Burley, and 3-4 old guys talking about World War II.

Well, after lunch I was sitting there with Buddy, and this fella come in, kind of odd-looking in that he's got glasses on, and one lens is clear and the other dark. I didn't ask what that signified, as I didn't want to pry. He sat down on the barstool next to me, looked at me and Buddy, nodded and said, "I'll bet you a beer I can stick a 8-penny nail up my nose."

I said, "Say what?"

He looks past me to Buddy and says to him:

"This boy sell molasses? Has he got a case of the slows, or what?" Then he laughed, and Buddy laughed a little, too—though he told me later he just did it out of politeness.

I tried not to get too worked up about it. I've stood accused all my life in this town of being just a hair off, mainly because of the slow way I speak. Still, I'm a little sick of it. So I went to my truck and got a 8-penny nail out of the toolbox.

And damn if he didn't stuff that nail all up in his nose.

It impressed the hell out of me. He got everybody else in the bar on that bet, then later, three golfers came in, and he snookered them for a six-pack. I even walked over to the gas station and got a couple of the boys there to come and witness it.

Finally I asked him, "Can you do a 10-penny nail?"

He didn't allow he could do that.

I said, "Why not?"

And he replied, "That might hurt."

"Can you wait here a minute?" I asked. "I want to go fetch my girlfriend, so as she can see you do that."

He said, "Whyn't you do that then." And he added, "It'll cost her a beer." Then he tilted toward Buddy, raised his eyebrows, tapped his forehead and said to me, "G o o d B y e."

A real card.

I drove over to Dade City, 6-8 miles distance, to get my girlfriend, Mozell, and that's when the trouble started, as it usually does start with her it seems.

Mozell is almost exactly 11 years younger than I am. She's young and she's wild. I used to drive truck for a living. I hauled oranges for Lykes-Pasco. But after my folks passed away, since I then owned about half of Michigan Avenue in San Ann, two houses, an orange grove, pole barn, Airstream trailer, and a hodgepodge of outbuildings and sheds, I saw no further need for gainful employment. So about two years ago I retired. And though I enjoy the lifestyle, when hunting season ends, I often find myself on the lookout for activities to fill my time. Mozell sort of fit the bill. She was like a hobby I took up. My only other hobby then was drinking so much I was seeing double every night driving home from the bar.

Now Mozell, to me anyway, is quite attractive, though my tastes might differ from yours. She's got some Cherokee in her. She has two long elbow-length plaits, one on each side of her head, jet black in color, and high cheekbones. She has, also, a thyroid condition, and her eyes are very large and come out toward you. They are so big and strange, I find them exotic. They are glossy and a deep and dark shade of brown, and, like I say, they're hard to miss.

Now I've been encouraged by the Professor to tell all sides of the truth in this, to be frank with myself also, etc. So, take Buddy, he thinks of Mozell as "bug-eyed and somewhat a pig." His words, not mine. But, you ever see a wild hog rooting, they dig with their noses, using it like a shovel, and, actually, I think a hog is beautiful, though most people believe hogs to be ugly. But I'll tell you, if you watch a hog in the wild you will see a side of a hog you've never seen before. But this is beside the point.

The point is, when I first ran into Mozell, she had a boyfriend already, and his name was Snapper. I won't give his last name. But that's his legal Christian first name. The two of them came in the bar one night, this is 9-10 months back. Snapper goes 6'4", 270, no fat. He don't lift weights but looks like he does. First time I saw them in there, PeeWee's sitting beside me, I said to Snapper, jokingly, "This guy's name is Mr. P. Wee, and he'd like a fight with you." Snapper says, not even looking our way, "Why don't you and him both go outside, get started without me. I'll be there in a minute." Then he drank down his Busch, crushed the can against his temple, and laughed like a nut.

Well, I had to hand it to him on that one, as I thought it was pretty damn funny. But he's got Mozell with him, and later on she gives me the eye.

Now, like I said, Mozell's eyes are sizeable. And when she gives you the eye, there's no getting around or denying the fact, and of course, Snapper noticed it, too, and hasn't thought well of me since—though I don't believe he likes anyone too much to begin with.

So that time, I told Mozell, "Thanks all the same."

Like I'm not interested. But of course I was.

At the time, Snapper was employed at the Auto Salvage Yard in Lacoochee. I started thinking on how I could work around this, if you get my drift. But these two was like a knot you couldn't untie. I thought for weeks on how I could get her shed of him, but nothing good occurred to me wherein I could do that and avoid getting killed in the process. Because don't get me wrong, Snapper was a hardass from the word go. Hearsay had it he just hatched mean and has been that way ever since.

Then one morning, I was out on my porch swing having some grits and cheese mixed up for breakfast when Hiram Bucklew pulled into the yard with a dead coyote on the fender of his Chevy truck. Hiram was one of my Daddy's buddies. He's retired now and hunts foxes and coons, which are pests everyone wants to thin out anyways. This old truck he'd bought new in '53, and it still don't have a hundred thousand miles on it. He had three of his hunting dogs in the truck bed and his black Lab in the shotgun seat—the Lab is all but a member of the family, having moved above dog status—and that's when I got my idea.

You see, Hiram's crazy about dogs. He raises his own hunting dogs and can quote you the genealogy (the Professor gave me this word—he has also corrected my grammar and spelling, though he said, otherwise, he would subtract none of what he called "the color" from the story) of his present dogs going back to the first one his father gave to him during The Great Depression, names and dates. And I've kept in touch with him since Daddy passed. Daddy was helped across by his drinking and smoking habits, and Hiram witnessed much of it through the years. He sometimes now gets confused over Daddy's name and mine and refers to me as Hank. But he's just a good guy. During hunting season, say I get a hog or deer, I'll take the innards over to give to his dogs—the heart and liver, the lungs, what I call "the lights"—especially if he's got puppies, chop all that up and give to the puppies that don't hunt yet. It makes them hungry for wild things.

But anyways, after we got done bullshitting, looked over his coyote and heard the story of its undoing (coyotes are still somewhat a rarity here, though they're moving into the area), made him some grits and all, I related to Hiram about the dog fights I'd heard of up in Sumter County, which Snapper was involved with, had a dog fighting in, as he is a gaming type. Acted like I'd been there. Told a story, you might say. (I'm of two minds on this lying business, but anyhow. . . .)

"That dog a Snapper's won its bout," I told Hiram. "Wadn't much to look at. Had a big ole head, but . . ." I trailed off.

Hiram said, "But what?"

I said, "Well . . . it wadn't no regular dog that day."

Hiram said, "What you mean, Monroe, it wadn't regular? Was it a talkin' dog or somethin'? Said, Give me some backstrap? I want soupbones?" He thought that was clever and went on in this vein for awhile. "Did he ask for a raise?" On and on.

"No," I said finally, "Snapper had fed it gunpowder."

Then he got my point. Now you can make any male dog meaner'n hell with a little gunpowder in its food, but the practice is cruel, among other things, such as being against the law. And Hiram got fired-up about it right then and there and later went home and reported the dog fights to the Sheriff, a friend of his. I think maybe they're even related in a roundabout way. This is not unusual. There's 500 people live in San Ann, and every other one of them is kin to me of some sort.

But Snapper spent a night in jail behind that. Then the *Tampa Tribune* picked up the story somehow, and he was in and out for awhile. He'd be out two days and back in the third, and pretty soon I heard that he'd left town and, in so doing, became a fugitive from justice. So I made my move on Mozell.

Come to find out, she didn't give a damn about Snapper. She was just petrified of him. Turns out her real love is yours truly (though Buddy Stortch, as is his way, says this is only because she found out about the property I own—but then he's got an opinion on every damn thing—I mean, it's his right—this is a free country, or used to be anyway. But let's get back to the story).

And here's where it gets complicated and makes me wonder if this writing business isn't harder than it looks. Because for the past six weeks people had kept coming up to me saying things like, "Monroe, I saw you down at County Line Bar Friday night. Man, you were a mess. I never seen you quite like that before." Or, "I come up to you at the Quaker Bar (in Dade City) the other night and said 'Hey' and you didn't even acknowledge me. You mad at me for some reason?"

This Mex I know named Roy St. Rio, he comes to the bar one night, mad as hell, says, "My old lady tell me you pinched her ass down in Trilby town." I mean I had used to work with Roy at Lykes, and he knew me and knew I wouldn't do such a thing. Still, here he was in my face.

Then one day I got a phone call at home. I picked it up and a female voice immediately demanded to know where I'd been. The voice didn't sound familiar.

I couldn't place it even as a vague acquaintance. She said her name was Stroud and that she was Wanda's sister. She chattered on 3-4 minutes. I really hadn't heard a word of it, still trying to figure out who she was. Finally, she asked if it would be okay if her Dad came to take back Wanda's things. I'd just returned from lunch and was about half in the bag. The whole thing struck my funnybone. "Certainly," I said. "Would 5 o'clock be convenient?" Right before she hung up she said, "I just want you to know, I think you're the sorriest son of a bitch in the history of bullshit."

I swear to God I have no earthly idea who Wanda Stroud is.

One day at the gas station I was talking to my cousin Burley and Cliff Pike, just leaning against Burley's tow truck there trying to explain this dilemma, and Cliff, he's Junior Pike's nephew, said, "Damn, Monroe, maybe you got a dark twin you don't know about out there doin' your dirty work for you."

Well, let's move past this. I didn't understand it at all, but it has to do with what happened later this day.

I'm beginning to detect, at this point in the story, that my writing style bears a close relationship to my Daddy's way of never throwing anything out, whether it was worth keeping or not.

The little house where I'm now living is the house where my mother grew up. My parents' house is the next one up the street. It's a large white house, seven rooms on the bottom floor and five on the second story. Some years back it got so crowded with antiques Daddy had bought at flea markets and such over the years, they just moved out, came down to the place I am now, as my Aunt Arlene, who had lived here alone forever, in her 67th year of life found a boyfriend at last and moved into Dade City with him. The big house is still sitting there as my parents left it. You can barely make your way through it for all the strange objects collected therein.

Anyhow, I drove to Dade City, then north on 301 a bit to pick up Mozell. Her mama has a fruit stand there, and Mozell lends a hand in the afternoons. Her mama is skinny and cranky and is not friendly towards me at all. They sell fruits and vegetables, eggs, fishing worms, sodas, and a bunch of Mexican products—chorizo, jalapenos, pinto beans, Mex cassette tapes, etc. On the side of the stand there's a painting of a basket of fruit tipped over and fruit falling out. They even have a Mexican parrot somebody gave them speaks Spanish. Her mama lets that bird drink Jack D. out of a shot glass and watches it fly around and run into the walls for entertainment. Did I tell you I got no use for her?

But now, soon as Mozell gets in the truck, I see that she's not in the best of moods. I said, "I've missed you, baby." She didn't know what to make of such eloquence from me, I guess, and told me to fuck off. I hadn't been around for a couple days. I do this on purpose sometimes. Mozell's like a really good hot sauce—the longer it sits the hotter it gets. But like I say, she's young, and there's just no precise landmarks to go by with her. Also, she's got a bad temper and it can get away from her, so I don't like to get her too mad because she carries boxcutters in her purse.

We stop at a Circle K down the road. She says she needs a beer. I give her $5.00, and she returns with a six-pack and had finished off the first one by the time she's back to the truck. And she kept the change. Tells me to pull out of the sun under some oak trees beside the store. She says, "I caught a buzz 'fore you came. I need to settle my nerves."

When she mentions that word, I clam up. I just don't want to hear about it. The strongest substance I do is horseradish, and she's out of my league in this business.

She comes into the bar not long ago with a Mason jar of 'shroom juice, tells Burley it's ice tea, only a little different, try some. After awhile Burley goes, "Whoa!" grabs hold of the bar with both hands. "Damn," he says, "this whole place is about to capsize, ain't it?" For some reason, he thinks this is just about the funniest damn thing he's ever said, and shortly thereafter falls off the barstool from laughing so hard.

I mean, Burley's crazy anyhow, he don't need no outside help. Later on he starts up his tow truck, hitches a chain to a big palm tree behind the bar, yanks it out of the ground by its roots, and starts driving around town with it. The State Patrol stopped him in front of the post office. How do you explain something like that?

But now we're sitting under the shade of the trees, and Mozell shoots down two more beers. I'm weighing mine in my hand, and it's just over half empty. She cracks another. It loosens up her mood, though, and she slides over by me and starts fooling around. She's lively that way.

There's some Mexicans in a blue Plymouth pull up close by to our left, four lowriders. They're just staying out of the sun, too. The guy in the shotgun seat goes into the store. Mozell pops the last beer, looking past me to the Mexicans, trying to stare them down or something. Then she starts fussin' about them, saying this and that. Starts getting louder at it. "I would stop right there," I said, but she paid me no mind. She knows all kind of bad language, too, and now she's keen on practicing it.

All of a sudden she says loudly toward their direction, "*Pendejo!*" (This means something like dingleberry, and I've noticed the Mex don't care for it in the least.) And she screams out, "Did everybody hear that?" Although, truth be owned, I don't think them boys, till she yelled at them, had even noticed us, other than to admire my truck perhaps. Then she screams at the top of her lungs, "What you starin' at? This ain't no pitcher show! Ain't no drive-in-movie thee-ate-ter!"

The driver, he don't respond in words. He goes straight to his trunk, takes out a sawed-off and jacks it. And I'm out a there.

I don't mind a fight. I'll throw up my set anytime. But you get into firearms, I think discretion is the best course. For all I know of these Mexicans, hell, they might be head hunters. I believed I could lose them, too, because I knew that car. It was a Plymouth Horizon with a Dodge Omni 2.2 turbo engine in it. Junior Pike had built it years back to race with. Later it belonged to a fella in San Ann named Mingo, who ran it into the ground. And who knows who's had it since. Still, it took me awhile, and I had to pull a trick I knew on Bull Road before I lost them.

Only trouble is, it's clear to me they could surely recognize my truck in the future. It's flame red and kind of distinctive-like with its pin-striping. And also, they'd taken a good look at me. They were pretty much just seeing me, and hearing Mozell's nonsense.

I went to my place. Mozell sat down in a chair in the living room, gave me a sidelong look. She closed her eyes momentarily, then opened them big and turned toward mischief. She had on a short skirt and sat there with her legs carelessly apart, and I took her just like that in the chair. We didn't hardly remove our clothes. We taught that chair some tricks—taught it how to stand up on its hind legs. But afterwards I had to take some Goody's powder for the headache the whole incident had given me.

I fear I lack my Daddy's fortitude in dealing with women. My mother lasted a year without him, then started talking about how he had called her—a connection, apparently, with some static on the line. Which was her way of saying, I think, that he was still speaking his mind.

After putting my truck in the barn and switching to Daddy's Ford van for any further travel, I took Mozell home. I'd had enough of her for one day.

There's this old fart comes in the bar, goes on about how the world would be a whole lot better place to live in if there was open season on women, at least one day of the year. I wouldn't go that far myself. But women are a study. They just seem to be a different critter entirely, one I'll never fully understand, no matter how long I hunt them, especially those like Mozell, who are stone crazy in the mind, throwing so many shapes around you don't know which to take for the real one, and yet got that sweet body that makes you long for them. You're dancing with the devil on your back there, to quote a phrase.

I got some gas for the van and stood around bullshitting with the boys at the Shell station awhile. It was near dark and kind of pretty out, as the sun and the moon were both in the sky. I drove over to the bar and pulled up under some trees off to the west side, turned the van so that it was facing Route 52. I was thinking, This has been a memorable sort of afternoon. Then I looked toward the bar.

There's a pay phone near the front door. A fella was dialing a number. I did a double-take on him. The guy looked just like me. He had the same build, hair color, three-day beard. He's got on a camouflage ballcap, like I always wear. If I didn't know any better, it was me.

As he's dialing, then starts talking, I see that Plymouth Horizon pull up to the bar down the way. Sits there awhile. Then backs up and pulls in front of the pay phone. Three Mex pile out and start knocking the shit out of this guy. He didn't know what hit him. They were still working him over as I pulled away. I didn't have any pressing need to make a call right then and had been thinking, anyhow, maybe I should cut back on my drinking, at least one night of the week.

But from what I saw they did to that boy, it was like the fella said about the 10-penny nail—looked like it might hurt.

A Small Thing That Mattered Greatly

Louie Sorrels lived on the top floor of the hotel. The roof was made of tin, and when the wind rattled it, his room had a metallic voice. He slept with his clothes on and his coat, so in the morning he wouldn't have to dress in the cold. When the voice woke him, he got out of bed and started walking. He walked to the nearest cafe that was open, ordered coffee, and sat by the stove. He held the cup with both hands. He watched through the window people walking by exhaling frost.

Later he stood outside and counted his change. This did not take long. His third day in Tampa, Louie's wallet had been lifted. But he did not report this to the law. He'd just built three years at Starke Penitentiary, and the thought of cops made him sore. The dark rooms with their feminine odor that told him stories about life were suddenly out of range. His sister had to wire money from Dothan, Alabama, but it brought bad weather south with it, and the five twenties felt like a cold hand.

But Sweet Louie Sorrels was a man known to bet with scared money. He'd drifted down Nebraska Avenue that day to the dog track and bought tickets until he no longer had enough dough to leave town. For lunch from then on he would go to the Spanish restaurant on the corner and look through the window at the goldfish in the aquarium. If this did not satisfy him, he'd walk to Robles Park and watch the ducks in the pond. Children threw bread to them. The ducks were so fat they would watch it sink. For dinner, Louie drank beer. By this he filled his days and made his clothes grow bigger.

Louie counted his change. His reflection did not take part in this but stood aloof, its dark olive skin marked by cartoons drawn on the window by children. It looked around in embarrassment. The black hair combed straight back was too rich for this, the high cheek bones too proud. Its eyes flashed like a blade being pulled. When Louie turned in the direction of a bar where the waiter sometimes spoke kindly, his reflection felt no longer bound to him, and made its own way down the windowpanes of Ybor City.

As Louie walked, the wind blew across him. It was this morning like a little girl with old clothes on who had never cut her hair.

"Give me a beer," Louie said to the waiter.

The waiter was polishing the taps. He looked at his watch.

"You want a large glass or a short one?"

Louie looked at the glasses. They were all the same size.

"What's the difference?"

"With a large glass you get conversation."

"Loan me some jack," Louie said.

"What you're lookin' for is a short beer," the waiter answered.

While the waiter banked the fire in the woodstove, a young man entered the bar and sat at a table against the wall below a vase of blue flowers that were falling asleep. He was thin and angular and dressed all in black, with blond hair and smoking eyes. He looked at the waiter and Louie and at the little faces in the fire, and the room relaxed.

He ordered coffee and a brandy.

Outside the windows the city had woken and now moved against the cold. People walked with sleepy faces, eyes slanting up or down or straight across with lines fanning from the corners as they squinted. Children did not chase candy wrappers down the street but walked like grandfathers in order not to be strangled by wind and soot. Red shirts and dresses stood out but everything else was gray or dark yellow, and everybody was too close to something.

"Are you from here?" the young man suddenly asked.

As he spoke, two Cuban women dressed in mourning walked by the window arm in arm. There was much of that around, Louie had noticed, ancient women who dressed in black every day of their lives. Ybor City is the old Latin quarter of Tampa. Louie was here because rooms were cheap. He shook his head.

"Is it cold where you are from?"

"Why?" Louie answered.

"For this is nothing. In my country the snow must now squeak underfoot. And the fields are blue in the morning. But I have been gone too long. When I look back, it's not me anymore. It is only a child there."

"I ain't been gone so long," Louie said.

"But if you went back, even now," the young man said, "they might not recognize you. People change who go away. That is why it is important to learn the ages of those who go away, in order to tell how old they are when they return."

"I got other things on my mind," Louie said.

"As do I," the young man said and put his hand to his forehead. "And my thoughts won't quit talking of it."

"I don't know about that," Louie said. "What I know is I ain't eat good for a couple, three weeks."

The young man took a sweet roll from a brown bag that was soaked through with sugar.

"You must try this. It is called *Gypsy's Arm.*"

When Louie took the first bite, he just closed his mind a moment there.

"Look," he said, "I'm just eatin' this food. It's good food, and I'm eatin' it. Pretty soon it'll be gone. . . ."

"You owe me nothing. Finish it, please. My mother made it. Perhaps just for you."

"How would she know me?" Louie asked. But the young man did not seem to hear him.

The young man's name was Misha. He spoke of the circus and of Lithuania. He spoke into noon. Now they sat on a bench in a little park between two avenues.

"In seven days," Misha concluded, "meet me here in the evening. I will take you to a place where you can have all you want to eat."

"Go on," Louie said in disbelief.

*

During the early part of the week, in preparation for Gasparilla, Tampa's Carnival celebration, workmen spread colored lights above the streets, and the foot traffic grew into crowds at dusk. Each night the crowd grew larger. There was perfume in the air, the odor of burnt sugar and spoiled oranges, and the moon each night had another woman's face.

The people resembled gourds in their coats, Louie thought. He took to pasting magazine pictures of food on the walls of his room. He hung around the market place and took deep breaths. Each day he passed the park bench in awe. It was wonderful and yet so uncertain. He began to make up little lies. One was the notion that the mere thought of something could cause it to happen. At night he dreamed of food, and in the morning he was full; he could hardly move. But after the third day there came a whispering in his nerves. And sometimes this was like when the stars first come on at night, but other times they sparked like fish out of water.

The next evening he returned to the hotel and discovered that his room had been switched without notice. He had just shoplifted a bottle of port in a little store and was quite proud of this. He had thought himself all but invisible doing so, completely unaware that every person in the place had seen him take the wine. He had such a feral look about him, they simply closed their eyes to it. When he returned to the hotel, the night clerk was not at his station. There was a bowl of hard candy on the desk. Louie emptied the candies into his coat pocket and went to his room, only to find an elderly Cuban gentleman occupying it. He was giving himself a shave at the time, a towel over one shoulder.

The old man was polite and spoke at some length, trying to clear up the situation, but not a word of it was in English. Neither was the night clerk particularly fluent in his explanation. He showed Louie to his new room, which was just down the hall. Louie's belongings had been stuffed into a paper grocery bag and sat on the bed. The night clerk gave him a new key. Even more incomprehensible, he then stood there for some moments as though desiring a tip.

"Yeah . . .right," Louie said.

Louie looked around. This room was as derelict as the other. It looked identical as a matter of fact. After he finished the wine, he fell down several times to keep things lively. Then he sat on the bed and started on the candy. He studied the room. No matter how long he regarded it, however, he could not shake the notion that this was the same room he had just been moved out of.

He grew impatient. The night before the seventh day, a spider came down from the spokes of its web and crossed Louie's game of solitaire. Louie's sense of smell was now acute. Fragrances surrounded him. Some were delicate and seemed afraid to let him come to know them. But the hallway was strong with vomit and backwash from the toilets.

Sleep this night was a kind of falling—into a dream that in the morning he could not remember. Then the day passed. He couldn't tell you how.

As the sun went down, his shadow became long and thin and stood off to one side. Louie sat on the park bench and watched the evening maneuver into place. He was no longer certain what he looked like. The mirrors had become too glamorous and would not look back.

He glanced down the street toward the bar. *Come now,* he thought, *come talk to me. Make it that the night does not move so.* For there had begun little accidents in his nerves. He thought of his hunger then as a woman, a lover that had stopped talking to him, who was far away and yet closer than anything he could touch. The cold no longer bothered him and not the hardness of the bench. He thought only of what a fool he had been. For a promise between strangers was but a small thing.

And now it was difficult to get anywhere, for though he walked toward the bar, it receded at an equal pace before him. But when he stopped to rest he was suddenly at the door, and then he sat on a stool, and, without quite knowing how it happened, there was whiskey in his shaking hands. It soon rambled through his veins. He looked around. Men of all types sat or stood along the bar, and without exception, each of them was spilling his drink. He had only been situated on his stool for a short period of time, and not knowing why they spilled half of what they drank, he at first presumed they were careless, and was annoyed. But after the first drink, Louie began to spill himself.

Now every time a glass was lifted, much of the beer and liquor spilled out, rolling down chins and onto the bar. The splattering of raw beer and whiskey hit the floor. It was slightly amusing—the taps were flowing, and the men at the bar spilled their drinks with a sense of pride, but constant stares and snickering in his direction made the smile on Louie's face sometimes falter.

He tried several times to engage the man to his left in conversation. He was a tall man with a blank expression on his face. Both times the man had turned his head to gaze at Louie and, shortly thereafter, commenced doing bird imitations. After the second rebuff, Louie shouted to the bartender, "How about another?" and pointed to his glass. At this the fella to his right, who up till then had kept his face averted, burst into such convulsive laughter he could not catch his breath, until finally he spun his stool around and kicked his legs in the air in shameless hilarity. Louie looked at his glass again, and, to his amazement, it was full. He tried to take one more drink but spilled it all down him. And though he meant to only put down his glass, he saw instead that he had opened the door, and the street flowed before him. There across it stood Misha, waiting.

"Where's that food . . . or was you just talkin'?" Louie said, and he closed one eye so that Misha would come into focus.

They walked through the crowd, which grew or lessened, but acted always like there was something funny going on. And there came a street where they no longer had to walk but which seemed to move them along as if they were going somewhere. Now the circus stood before them, and they entered the big tent. There was no audience. And the emptiness of the seats looked around and acted sad. Inside the wooden ring, three long tables groaned from the weight of the food and bottles on them. The circus performers were having a feast, and they were all in costume. Mirrors set around the ring made the people endless, and some were funny mirrors, and people walked away from them distorted. Apples and grapes rolled off the tables, and the bears ate them, and the lions were curious. Food spilled from the tables, and the clowns walked in it and the big feet of the giant, and Louie stood there saying a prayer of thanks he had learned as a child.

Before him were spreads of pickled herring, smoked salmon, lamb and goose. There was red and white wine, and cranberry dessert with little cookies called

Slizikai, dipped in sweet water. Louie ate and became ridiculously drunk. He ate more, and he was a hit with the ladies from the kitchen. He ate enough for the week, for he knew luck would not strike in the same place twice.

"What's this?" he asked drunkenly.

"Pisht," Misha answered. "Blood soup."

Louie was next seen bent spasmodically over a pile of sawdust, several transvestites nearby giggling.

But even in his drunkenness, he was amazed at how his friend was taken here. The stars paid their respects to Misha. And something else was going on, too—something darker and underneath it all. The juggler came up to Misha and said, "I'm sorry about Tino. But maybe it is for the best." The strongman cried at the mention of this name. And the wife of the acrobat said, "God will make him better now." The barker agreed. And the two greyhounds at the feet of Louie Sorrels turned their heads.

Now he wondered about Tino but dared not ask, for he saw those concerned look at one another with death in their eyes.

"What'll they do with all this?" he asked. "Maybe I should put some in my pockets, so it don't go to waste."

"The leftovers will be taken by the children and fed to the animals," Misha said. "The hay under the tables will be taken also. The children have drawn straws from it to see who among them will live the longest. I did this many times when I was little. At midnight the animals talk to the children and thank them, but we were always too sleepy by then to listen."

"I take some a this . . . it'll lighten their load," Louie continued.

Misha answered. "My mother is waiting."

As Misha walked away, something inside of Louie seemed to leave, also. And just then, a bear that had been around stood up beside him and started mumbling.

Outside the big tent the wind blew hard, changing the scene around until Louie fell. Misha sat him in an angle of light against the wall of a courtyard, and spoke to him in a voice not quite his own.

"My mother's name is Nidute Mazeika. She was born in the village of Jodenenai, Lithuania. When I was still young, because my mother had seen soldiers crossing into her dreams, we journeyed to a holy city, whose name I am forbidden to mention. We lived in a house with three windows. In one was the Black Sea. In another the Sea of Azov. In the third window, beyond the room that waited hopelessly for my father—and let me say, there was a rainbow in this room from my mother's crying—there were mountains that, to me when I was little, sailed against the sky. It was a beautiful and sad place. Five times a day the muezzins called the faithful to prayer. That this was the prison of five towers became a joke that passed among us.

"In time my mother began to speak words that were out of keeping with her pride. My family, and by this I mean all who ate at our table, labored under her displeasure. One morning in a mountain village, she watched a child make an angel in the snow. She attached to this a significance I could not understand. The next three days she spoke in tongues. Those who understood her, it made blind; those who did not understand could only wonder. But on the night of the third day, Ksavaris the Dwarf first noticed Tino in the pocket of her apron. Even then he was no more than a doll. I can't describe Tino; you would have had to see him. But he knew how to get from place to place. He traveled light. He got there ahead of time. And he led us out of the hostile city, across the winter, to a small house by the sea. We stayed there only a few hours before we sailed to the new world, but the mirrored walls saw the hardships we had faced. The journey had taken many lives, and some of those who were now dead did not yet know it.

"As Tino aged, he got smaller as his value to my mother grew less. Finally his voice became too weak to hear. These past months, my mother had to put little pieces of gold in the pockets of his sweater to hold him in place. To complicate this, there are others who seek my mother's favor. There are many. It is my belief that one of these took the gold from Tino's pockets—and one morning, not so long ago, the wind blew him away."

Louie noticed now that his shadow abandoned him and starting picking the flowers that grew in pots along the courtyard. And he started laughing, like a man will when a joke has been told and he doesn't know whether or not it's on him.

"Enter," Misha said, and he motioned toward a small tent which appeared before them. "She is with her fool, Mecis, and should be in good spirits. If not, give way to her, even in matters of no importance. . . .

"Mama," he said, and his mother turned her great bulk toward them.

She wore black silk with a border of gold embroidery. An ankle bracelet sparked when she moved. Her hair was long and so light it was a color nobody could explain, but she was blue under the eyes and her smile dark and mocking.

She needs a butcher, Louie thought, and he paid her little mind, though he wondered how in the world they moved her. He measured the doorway with his eyes and concluded there was no way she could get through it.

Now from a dark corner, the fool, Mecis, uncoiled himself and stood. He was dressed in rags and drunk in the eyes, and, as he moved, straw fell from his sleeves.

Scarecrow, Louie thought, and he stepped back in alarm.

"Is this the lamb?" asked the fool.

"I notice your sense of humor is still broken," Misha answered.

"Do not align your voice against me," the fool warned. "Your words might turn upon thee. There is a sharpness in that you have not yet known, and it cuts from far away."

The two of them spoke in a language completely foreign to Louie. But now in English, "I have seen this one pass through the city," the fool said, pointing to him, "like a cop watching people. Mark my words. They're worth their weight in gold."

"Aye," Misha said, "fool's gold."

"An old fool, too," Nidute Mazeika suddenly spoke. "Do not play his game. It will profit you nothing. On the night he was conceived, a goat looked in his mother's window."

Out of nervousness, Louie picked up a shell that was lying at his feet, the kind that has the ocean in it, but he put his ear to it and heard laughter.

"Yeah," Louie said, to no one in particular, "that's good, that's a good one." And he laughed too, though in truth he couldn't make head nor tail of what was happening.

"Whenever something good happens," the fool said, "I thank God, and curse the devil because he wasn't around when I wanted to get it from him."

Without saying another word, he left, though he made a big production of his going. He became a mime, and there were several invisible doors to contend with before he found the outside. Seemingly caught up in this, Misha tipped a hat that he did not actually wear, bid his mother and Louie goodnight, and went away.

To add to Louie's discomfort, however, when he glanced out the doorway the flowers all turned their heads to look at him.

Then the lady called Nidute Mazeika said something odd.

"I have two names," she said. She smiled at this, and her eyes contained a faraway thought, until she was not the same any longer. As if a smile could bring back beauty from another time, she was now thin and spoke with the silliness of a young girl who has just discovered her beauty, and how attractive she is to men. Or again, her body was lovely as a woman so newly pregnant she had not yet told anyone. And they were not where they had been anymore, but went falling through events that happened too fast to keep up with.

Then they were lying near a river, like an indigo ribbon, where fish broke the surface of the water and turtles arranged themselves like steps across. In the distance there was a prospect of plain and hill, though nothing was certain but that which was close, willows sobbing into the shade below them, the lament of the river that offered its arm to an ancient sea.

As Louie watched the moments revolve around him, he could not move but only listen.

"Here time has no bearing," she said. "Or perhaps it is that endless row of orchids that strangers admire so much.

"Years ago when I was young and already weary of the Earth, suddenly everything was far away. The place where I had been was so small I could hold it in my hands. The place I arrived at I knew nothing of. It was out of the current of the world I had known.

"On that grass road to the west, I came upon a man who was beautiful and strong. He talked to me but never spoke. I asked that he not reveal he had seen me. In answer he motioned toward the thousands of people who now lined the road, sitting with their eyes closed. He was so attractive I wished that I were older. He leaned down and kissed me, and I aged seven years. As we walked along afterwards, I knew without being told what he wanted. He came so close to me, I thought only that I was riding my own body. He did this to me twice. Once for me, and once for the little girl I had been. And the second time I carelessly let go of the reins.

"My son came of this, though on Earth it took him seven years to be born. I have seen it happen many times since. When two meet who are destined for each other, they begin a spiritual child. . . ."

Before she could finish, however, a strange bird landed near them, a species unknown to Louie. It hopped around Louie and looked him up and down.

"Is it a worm?" the bird asked.

"No."

"Is it a seed?"

"No."

"What then is its worth?" the bird asked. It squawked and flew away.

She called after it: "There's something I must say. . . ." But the bird went to the river and drank of the winding mirrors and shadows, then perched on a nearby tree and turned its back to them.

"He is beautiful, don't you think? But his moods," she said. "I believe in his last life he must have been a Spaniard. On Earth he was difficult to explain. Something was lost in the translation. He was small to begin with, and, from time to time, parts of him would migrate, until he became so little he could no longer hold his place there. And his hair often changed color with the seasons. No one knew what to make of it."

She turned her face to his now and kissed him. And though he did not return this, it gave movement to his voice and body. He looked around for a way out.

"Do not try," she said. "There are angles here from which you cannot escape."

"Why have you brought me here?" he asked.

"Because on Earth you did not look at me with enough curiosity. . . . No, that is not true. I thought that you might die in a place you did not have to."

He felt her touch then, deeper than he could follow.

"I am yours . . . but, please," she said, "do not bring me to that place in you that I cannot waken."

There, very close now, as he turned his mouth down upon hers, the one eye that Louie always kept open caught on the bird in the tree. The bird opened its tail, and the world he had known before this moment was lost in the design that spread across the horizon. . . .

And that is how they found Louie Sorrels, down in Ybor City, winking at death on a park bench in the morning.

The Gaffer

He was sitting on a bench in front of the travel agency in San Ann. He lived down the road a quarter mile, I knew, and he was resting there, as his legs were not good anymore. He was a very old man with a thoughtful gaze rendered eerie by a wandering left eye.

I knew something of him from hearsay, as in a small town you get to know all you want, and much that you'd just as soon not.

A storm had passed through a bit earlier. The rain had cooled what heat there was in this November afternoon, and the sky was pearl and grey. I stopped and offered him a ride. He folded the newspaper he'd been sitting on, folded it again to fit in one hand and got into the truck.

I knew that he was an ex-carnie. That he walked to the bar each morning—you'd see him lumbering down Curly Avenue with his hands thrust into his pockets—that he stayed there most of the day. I knew that he lived with his nephew, whom I was acquainted with, and that he owed this nephew money enough that the nephew was reluctant to ask him to move on, though he wanted to. His nephew worked for Publix at night and had a spare-time job fixing lawnmowers. Some years back, a lawnmower of mine caught fire and began spitting out parts, and I had taken it to this nephew to repair. I'd been there a number of times since.

The nephew was a good mechanic, and he liked to talk. The last time I'd seen him, he was concerned in that some of his tools had been disappearing. "I just hate to see things walk off like that," he'd told me.

Well I knew all this but said nothing, and the old man and I rode in silence to where he lived. I'd just been to the little store and purchased a six-pack, and it sat between us.

The old man had a rotund head, white hair clipped very short, a face mottled by age, high cheekbones, big shoulders and a bullneck. Though he seemed all rumpled and out of plumb elsewhere, his face was barely marked by timelines. He was wearing blue, Dickey work clothes, the shirt longsleeved, and Red Wing boots. A ball cap tilted to one side. Most of his weight seemed to be above the waist. You could see that he'd been a powerful man once, but now his body was played out. He kept clearing his throat, though not, apparently, to say anything. He seemed preoccupied, in the way drunks often are.

I pulled into the oyster shell driveway to the front of the house, a small, white, wood frame home with an open garage behind it, lawnmowers and parts spilling out, and his nephew's late model Ford truck parked alongside. The lawn, however, was little affected by this show of equipment and stood a foot tall.

It hadn't concerned the old man that I knew, without him directing me, exactly where to take him. I shook my head at him a couple times, as if to say, Well, here we are, but he just sat, looked the place over and didn't seem inclined to get out. We were parked under a live oak that was still dripping the rain.

Finally, holding up the newspaper, he said, "The Lobster Boy is dead. Did you know it?"

The Lobster Boy was one Grady Stiles Jr., 55 years old until a few nights previous when he'd been shot in the back of the head at his mobile home in Gibsonton, a little town south of Tampa where carnies live in winter. He'd been watching *Jeopardy* at the time. The victim had ectrodactyly, a genetic condition known as lobster-claw syndrome. His arms looked like claws and his legs were stumps. He had begun performing on the carnival circuit as a child and ultimately became owner of sideshows, including freak animals and the Gorilla Lady. He had been killed by a hitman, apparently hired by his wife. The hitman in this case being a neighbor kid. It had all been done so amateurishly even the cops figured it out. The story had been in both the *Tampa Tribune* and the *St. Pete Times* that morning. Said all that and some other things about it, too. The Lobster Boy's wife was claiming self-defense.

"I read about it," I said.

"The Lobster Boy was a friend of mine," the old man said. Then that haunted left eye landed on the bag between us like a moth and becalmed itself finally.

"You know," he said, "I could drink one a them, as I notice it is Busch beer, which is one of my favorites."

Hearing him talk now in that whiskey tenor, it was obvious he was already marinated, and what I had taken for moroseness on his part was only that he was a bit too high to be properly animated just now. So I said, "Sure." What the hell, I had nothing better to do. And turned off the ignition, and we opened one each and drank. At times a short one in such instances will bring on a second wind, and it wasn't long in coming.

"I'll pay you back one a these days," he said. "Right at the moment, I'm broke as the Ten Commandments, though."

"I know the feeling." I'd paid for the beer with small change, a quarter being my highest denomination this particular day.

"Did you know him long?" I asked. But he didn't get the drift of my question.

"Say again?"

"The Lobster Boy. You said he was a friend."

"Yeah, sure," he said. "I'm a carnie. You in that business, you know the Lobster Boy. But we was close, too. For a long time, anyway." And he added, "Not of late."

"What'd you do in the carnival?" I asked.

"I was a gaffer," he said. "An electrician. I was in charge of the lights. I kept the place bright. It was half the attraction, how we lit up the night in them little towns." He took a cigar butt out of his shirt pocket, stuck it in the corner of his mouth. He'd chew on it awhile, then put it back. "Then you do other shit, too. There's no end of something to do. An' you always on the move. It's what got me into the business—the travelin'. I was crazy for it when I was young."

"What was the Lobster Boy like?" I said. I'd seen the Lobster Boy once when I was a kid, and I remembered what he was like.

"Aw," the gaffer said, "Grady wasn't never far away from bein' no good. I always liked him anyways. I don't hold something like that to be so important.

We all assholes now and again. I worked for him from time to time. He never shitted me. He always leveled with me. You can't say that about everyone in the business. An' he was fun to drink with, least early on. I got torqued with him many a night. About the 11th hour of it, he'd turn awful sometimes. He just didn't seem to have any stamina for it."

I turned my head on that one. I thought maybe he was pulling my leg. But if he was, he deadpanned me on it. As he talked now, I noticed, maybe for the last time, that stray eye aimlessly roaming the world. Then I just seemed to forget about it.

"Grady liked to argue some," the gaffer was saying. "What else is a drunk supposed to do? It's part of the job. Especially in the winter. You can't set around having farting contests all the damn time. An' he had a propensity toward meanness then. Hell, you had all that shit wrong with you. . . ."

He stopped talking when a neighbor lady came out of the house next door. She was in her early 60's I'd guess, in a long, sleeveless black dress, her arms white and ropy, her red hair a sort of small explosion on her head. She had a cat on a leash, which was black also. She was a dreary item, one of San Ann's widows I knew had been picked up by the sheriff's deputies several years back one late night for wandering the streets with a live chicken under her arm, no further explanation or follow-up ever offered. People just shook their heads about it and went back to their lives. There was a rumor around that she had once been quite pretty. What happened to her beauty no one knew. Perhaps she had mislaid it.

She walked over to the property line and peered into the truck. The gaffer waved, but she wasn't having any of it. She screwed up one eye looking to see who I was. Satisfied as to my identity, apparently, she said now, "Don't believe a *goddamn* word he tells you." Also getting a comment in, the cat went "Miaow" rather sarcastically; then the old lady turned like a soldier and went back into the house, the screendoor banging behind her.

"Blame woman," the gaffer said. "She's a widow, you see. . . ." He said it like *widda*. "One night she gives me the 'come hither'; she hasn't forgiven me for it since. Afterwards, she told me she loved me. I made the mistake of sayin' in return, 'Thanks for the warning.' She's a little deaf. I didn't think she'd hear it."

He smiled then, a very wide, tight-lipped, a tooth here and there showing grin that was a thing strange to witness. A very close rendition of a wolf in good humor.

"These little towns," the gaffer said, looking around like this one was fast encroaching upon him, "I like movin' through 'em. This'n here, you ever notice, looks like everybody just got in from Dothan, Alabama, with a load of turnips."

He cracked another beer.

"Do you mind?" he asked then.

"No. Go ahead."

"What was I talkin' about . . . oh yes . . . Grady. See, he didn't mind running over your toes with his wheelchair if he was displeased with you. Hell, he had the disposition of a crawfish. But you don't find so many really *nice* people, say, in the business. Most of 'em I worked with was queer. . . ."

"Queer?" I said.

"Queer ain't the word. Queers and drug addicts. Not all of 'em, of course. There's some good ones. But it's a mean business.

"Here's one for you," he went on. "The Lobster Boy told me his old man woke him up in the middle of the night once . . . this was when he was 6-7 years old, mind you . . . his old man drunk as can be, down on his knees by the bed, swayin' back and forth there like an aquarium plant, and says to him, Grady, I'm gone to give you the secret word! Grady couldn't wake up. He said, What Daddy? The secret word goddamn you, and I want you to remember it the rest of your life. . . ." The gaffer took a long drink and fell silent.

"What word would that be?" I asked eventually.

"*Cunt,*" the gaffer said. "What else, right? But can you imagine? An' how was that boy ever to get any lookin' as he did. He went on the circuit soon after that. Went with the first carnival come through there and never looked back. They took him in and taught him the trade. He never went to school or nothin'. When I first knew him, he'd sign his name with a cross." The gaffer traced a + with a finger in the dust on the glove compartment. "What year truck is this?" he asked.

" '57."

"That was a good year," he said. " 'Course, Grady did find him a wife eventually, had kids an' all. But what kind a mean son of a bitch would parlay information such as that to his boy . . . it makes me feel very sorry for things . . . the Good Lord shuffled his feet on that one," the gaffer said, and crushed his beer can and chucked it onto the yard.

Once this was all over I said, "Did you know his wife?"

"Yes," he said. "She's a saint. She had to be to take him on in the first place. She ain't no beauty exactly." Then he waved a hand in front of him as if to erase these last words. "Mary's not someone I want to talk about. I wasn't brought up that way."

He began to rub his forehead with his right hand. Realizing in the process that his left hand was free, he reached over and got another beer with it.

"Drink a bit, do you?"

"Not as much as I'd like to," he answered.

He got to sniffing the air.

"This town smells like a wet dog when it rains."

The air smelled sweet to me, but I didn't say it.

"How old are you, son?"

"Fifty-one."

"You're young still."

"That's what my mother tells me," I said.

"I ain't cut out for old age," the gaffer said. "Or for hangin' around this sleepy-ass town. You know a damn cow walked down this street yesterday?

"I'm a travelin' man. I got it in my blood. I'll tell you . . . homely as I am, I used to do alright. I wasn't quite the sadsack lookin' fuck I am now, but I wasn't never no movie star either. I was a rascal, though, and the young girls liked that. Them good girls in towns up north. They are particularly decorative up there. Give their boyfriends a little tit, and say, Cut it out now! It was always hilarious to me. 'Cause with us, later in the night, things were different. They acted with abandon. They knew we'd be leavin' town soon. Somehow it made a difference. Them young girls give it all they've got, too. I can't say enough for 'em. Sometimes now at night, I dream of those times . . . and they come to me again.

"It's hard to believe it now, but, when I was a boy, there were still dray horses in the streets. Mules and wagons. Things have changed in my lifetime. The carnival changed, too. Freaks went out of favor, just like the girlie shows before had.

"Hell, any carnival worth its salt had a girlie show in the old days. It was one of the main attractions. For the men and boys at least. An' I mean, those were some sorry lookin' whores. I had to do creative work to light that stage favorably. Had to be almost starlight to make 'em look human. Blond wigs and red wigs, an' greyheaded pussies on 'em every one. Spavined . . . or skinny as knives . . . but mostly they were fat. Enormous. And it seemed like the bigger they were, the more emotional. God," the gaffer said, "I just hate it when the fat ones cry."

Very clearly then, from the kitchen window next door, the word "L I A R" floated out.

The gaffer looked over that way.

"Can she hear us talkin'?" I asked.

"No. She just says somethin' every now and then. Mox nix," he said. "No big deal. She still loves me. She just don't want to let on."

In a little while he said: "One thing about Grady . . . he had the goat's own root on him. Compensation, I guess. . . ."

I didn't care to get into how he knew this particular fact.

"I ran the Gorilla Lady show for him one summer. Just for a lark, really. I was the barker, too. It was hard to keep help. That monkey suit was hot. An' never was no "lady" involved. Just young winos. I finally found this boy liked to look up dresses. Before the show, he'd lay under the grate that led into the wagon an' shoot beavers. This was enough of an incentive for him to stay on. So that worked out good. But that winter, Grady bit off a fella's nose down in Gibtown, an' after that, I shied away from him some. . . ."

I went, "Nose?"

"Down at the Showtown Lounge . . . I think the two of 'em was playing checkers. Not a game of mortal violence usually. But this fella, Monk, said something untoward . . . I don't remember exactly what it was. Monk was a sap and a cornball." He said it like *cawnbaw*. "He said something that pissed Grady off. Grady jumped out of his wheelchair onto the table an' headbutted the guy. Them headbutts had some mustard on 'em, too, but they didn't seem to do fuck all . . . so he chewed Monk's nose off then. Spat it out like an olive pit."

"What'd Monk do?"

"He sued," the gaffer said.

A squirrel in the tree above us at this point began a convulsive barking, displeased with our station.

"I still got it," the gaffer said. "Wait a minute for me will ya?" He got out of the truck, stopped briefly and tried to locate the squirrel in the tree, then went into the house.

I was wondering to myself: Still got *what?*

Momentarily he returned with a peanut butter jar and a rawhide whip.

He handed me the jar and unfurled the whip and started circling the tree, peering up into it.

I sat there in the truck with the jar, looking at a piece of cartilage in clear liquid that appeared in all respects to have once been the end of somebody's nose.

When I looked up finally, the gaffer stood by the open truck door, in the corner it made, regarding me and winding the whip back into a circle.

"Can't reach him," he said, speaking of the squirrel. "I got me a rattler behind the garage last week. Popped his head right off. Blind luck, actually. I ain't proficient day to day with this yet." It was an old Cracker cattle whip and a nice one. "Separated that rattler from his head, an' it didn't even seem to notice. Kept on strikin'. Didn't have no head left, but he kept on. The knowledge caught up with him after awhile, though.

"I'd crack it for you, only it sounds like a pistol shot." He nodded toward the house. "I don't want to wake Vaughn." Vaughn McCaslin was his nephew's name.

The odor of cooking came from next door then, pots and pans being slammed around. The kitchenware and crockery seemed to be doing some nasty talking for her at the moment.

"Smell that?" the gaffer said. "She's always over there cookin' sausage." He left the door open but climbed back in the seat, his boots and lower pant legs soaked from the wet grass. He sorted through the six-pack.

"They's two left," he said. "Let's split them."

I set the nose over next to him. I didn't wish to study it any longer.

The squirrel barked and cooed some more.

"That damn squirrel don't like me," the gaffer said.

"I think," I said, "they just do that as a matter of course. I've never taken it personally myself."

He canted his head, looked at me like I'd really hit on something.

"No?"

I shook my head.

He cracked his beer and put down half of it.

"Good thing there's no law in this country against self-abuse," he said. "I want to thank you. I'm feelin' better . . . I feel good, damn it. I hate it when I have to take life seriously. An' it should never be so serious as to impact adversely on the drinking, is my way of looking at it.

"I only made one *big* mistake in my life. I mean, you make all kinds a little ones, right? They are endless. But the big one was, I just lived too long. I outlived my time. Otherwise, I got no regrets. I didn't do nothin' to merit it. Never took care of myself at all. It just turned out that way. I still got my own teeth. Most of 'em anyway. My own hair. There's a guy down at the bar wears this rug don't fit right . . . it jumps around on his head like a small animal. Who the fuck's he kidding? I still get a hard-on now and then. Jus' don't get many chances on it.

"But the trouble is," the gaffer said, "you stick around too long, it's bound to go sad on you. That's always the way of it. Life's just like any place." He finished the beer and wiped his mouth with the back of his hand. His hands were thick and gnarled and seemed older than all the rest of him.

"That last one'll set me up good for the night," he said.

"What you doin' tonight?" I asked.

"Nothin'," he said. "Then later I'm goin' to bed. . . . You from here?" the gaffer asked. He made a dismissive gesture with his hand, meant to encompass all of San Ann, I guess, like he'd just cast grain to some fowl.

"I live here now," I said. "I'm not from here."

"You *chose* to live here?" he said.

"Yes sir."

"Hmmm," he said.

"Where you from?" I asked.

"Right here," the gaffer said. "San Ann . . . I left this town when I was a boy. Never dreamed I'd be back."

Some distant musing took him then. He laughed quietly. He didn't look at me.

"Grady was a good man to drink with. So are you. It says something about a man. He was a happy go lucky fella then . . . what you laughin' at?"

"Says in the paper he killed his daughter's boyfriend with a 12-gauge," I said. "He'd had a few drinks. . . ."

"Oh," the gaffer said. "Yes, there's that. That was in '78. A bad year. Rained all the damn summer. He shot that boy up in Pennsylvania . . . it wasn't *down here,"* he said meaningfully, as if perhaps the latitude had put too much pressure on the trigger.

"Just a good-natured misunderstanding, I take it?"

"Not exactly," the gaffer said. "But you see, Grady only got probation for that now. Third degree murder. You know anything about the law, third degree tells you, in all probability, the son of a bitch deserved it."

There didn't seem to be any answer to that, and since the beer was done, I soon went on my way.

On the way home, I was trying to recall clearly the time I'd seen the Lobster Boy, one summer some 40 years past. The carnival came each July to the little town in northern Ohio where I grew up, and it was a big deal for us kids. Part of downtown was cordoned off and the carnival set up in the streets near the old high school.

I had never seen a freak before. I had, in fact, only recently eaten my first lobster at the local diner and had been such a hick as to ask where was the white meat on it, and where the dark? This brought some merriment to the waitress, who then, to my chagrin, shared it with all present. I was 11 years old that summer and just starting to learn that I really didn't know a damn thing.

I spent two nights of that carnival passing by the Lobster Boy's wagon but not going in. The third night, I put down my ticket and entered. There was a partition, waist-high, that made an aisle which took up about a fourth of the room. You went in one side, walked along this aisle, and out the other when you were done looking. It was like a very small and cheaply furnished motel room, and in retrospect it was simply that, his living quarters on the road.

The Lobster Boy was sitting on a table in the middle of the room. He had a dark towel over his extremities, naked from the waist up. Just by chance, I was in there alone with him. He had legs of some sort, but they didn't seem to be of any use. One ungainly foot protruded from beneath the towel. It looked something like his hands. He was barely a yard tall. His body seemed to have a gelatinous quality to it. We were eye level to one another. We regarded each other. He was more used to being stared at than I.

He was only four years older, but that thought never struck me until I read the account of his murder. It would have put him at 15 years of age that summer long ago, but there was no sense of time in years about him. He was an ancient being.

I found myself wanting to say something to him, I honestly don't know what. Just to be friendly, maybe. It was how you treated people in my town. You said hello, asked how they were doing, and so on. But when I looked directly into his eyes, I had the feeling that he was laughing at me.

The Lobster Boy reached over and picked up a pack of Lucky Strikes off the table with his right claw, shook out a cigarette and put it in his mouth. He picked up a Zippo lighter, which was beside an ashtray and a pack of Lifesavers. He lit the cigarette, shielding the flame with his left claw. He was not clumsy in any way about it. He inhaled deeply. Blue smoke.

"Go on," he said. "Beat it."

I was not fated to ever see the gaffer again after our conversation. His nephew, wanting to replace the tools he'd been losing, stopped at one of the local pawnshops that weekend, and, just by accident, came across a family heirloom, a silver-plated picture frame with a group photograph of his relatives from two generations back staring out at him. He said it seemed almost as if they were trying to catch his attention. Also in this pawnshop, he discovered two of his shotguns and a Colt.45 and holster his father had brought back from the Korean War; and the gaffer, soon afterwards, became a traveling man again.

Dream Rider

Gnats milled around me in the goldenrod. A spider climbed the air, and a catbird mewed. I watched the sun as it bled through the east—it caught on my body and my shadow awoke—and the direction I had to take unraveled the highway, a trestle and crossroads, and Memphis silhouetted in iron.

My luck spooked. I couldn't hook another car on my thumb. So I walked through the morning and the autumn into noon, where the day divided, and I saw the hours I had passed, and those yet stacked against me.

A man befriended me. He talked a good deal, and I talked too. I've noticed when people meet they are often afraid of silence because of what it could mean. His conversation had a strange, unstrung clarity to it—everything he said you could pocket—and after awhile I began to doubt him. He had a scar on his face that I looked at carefully, until once more it became the road I walked along.

I'm a little shaky. I've been doing this too much lately, inventing friends. I passed a yellow church, went down between the tall, square buildings, into the blue, monoxide valleys of traffic and noise. I found the bus terminal.

There was a bus scheduled for Paris, Tennessee, in an hour and a half. I thought of Paris; the old men smoking on the green; black ladies in flowered prints gliding by the storefronts in slow motion under umbrellas. The cotton would be picked now, and the corn, and talk would turn to the colors of the leaves, unless the politicians were in town.

The cafe next to the terminal served breakfast any hour. It was honky tonk, and no one noticed me enter. My appearance was way off. I'd gotten myself so thin down in Mexico, I blended into the scene.

A waitress sat near the counter in front of a fan that turned its face from side to side. I took a booth by the window, and she brought me coffee.

"Eggs and gravy," I said. "And some biscuit bread."

"The gravy's not but flour-water," she said. "It's not the best."

I looked at the specials on the menu.

"Give me the blue-plate, then."

Her smile gave away little jokes.

"You look like a real character, honey," she said.

While I was waiting for my order, a Harley pulled up alongside the window. There were two riders, dressed in t-shirts and denim. The big one in front turned his wrist, and the cycle growled. They wore black helmets and walked like confidence men, or insects—how a dragonfly will swagger in the air, or a mantis turn its head.

The one was tall and lean. He had a shaved head and a blue tooth; his eyes were hoods. There was in his expression a strange environment, like a place without weather, something left unasked, or that wouldn't echo; it was noble in a way, as in the time when the lords bred their children down the calendar without pity.

The posture of the other was very crooked. His hair was long, straw-yellow, electrical. When he talked, a lisp bit into his words, and vines of blood swung on his muscles. The big one ordered for him. He smiled, held a cigarette to his mouth, and smoke sewed the air.

The light swayed. I saw a man with the sun balanced on his shoulder. He lived in the window just a moment. He looked so much like me, as if I'd gotten separated from myself without knowing that I left.

The big one spoke once to his friend, called him Jack. Jack did not look up. He'd come across a red stone in the chili. His disgust got so heavy it had to take the chair next to him.

I left some change under my plate for the waitress. It wasn't enough, but I couldn't leave what I felt. She had been very nice. Perhaps I saw her going home by herself that night, somehow disappointed—not that she was alone, but that her hair smelled like smoke.

On the other side of the cafe was a bar full of queens. A mirror covered the back wall, and several of them were courting time there.

A man sat in the alley between the two buildings, his body in an angle of the sun, his face cut off by shadow. He had wrists like a little girl, and his hands quivered. There were two green bottles by him; one was empty and lay on its side, but the other was full and stood guard against hunger.

I asked about the Paris bus, down in a gaseous hallway lined with Greyhounds. One of the drivers said it was privately owned. That man over there said one thing, another said something else, and an old schoolbus, painted gray, and blistered by the seasons, drove out of the stories I'd been told.

Later, when we pulled out of the terminal, there were the two motorcycle hoods again, leaning against the cafe. They had toothpicks in their mouths. They were giving the bus the razor-boy look.

Though I am no longer awake, I'm telling myself the stairway I am on is not sleep. I confront my namesake and old tormenter. On the table before him is a bowl of oil, and light burning on a wick. The mirrors around him face the walls. It is necessary that he die so a tragedy might end. My .38 spoke, and he bowed to its eloquence.

I have slept with this dream many times, as I practiced my father's death. Often I would kill myself instead. To further this obscenity, I would die in the direction of love.

In the air around me are seven moons. Each one pulls me to a different course. Or are these the passengers I am now dimly aware of? My thoughts once more begin to take place in the world, the buildings of Memphis accelerating past the window.

An old man is driving the bus. He is cigar-skin, and has big, drawbridge eyebrows that raise and lower. His face is crazy with lines, as if he'd come undone somewhere else in his body.

Sitting behind him is a woman with a coarse voice. Her hair is tense. She studies an S&H Green Stamp Catalogue like the book of wishes, and draws on a long brown cigarette.

"April was the sweetest thing," she said. "I truly cared for her, I did. Till I started hearin' all them things people tolt about her. I should a knowed by them wigs she wore. Shorely she had to look so much nicer with her natchrul hair. He weren't no brother a hern neither . . . not that she ever confided understand . . . they was jus' complected diffurnt entirely. An' ever' day I'd bring her ice. I brung her Cokecola when I had . . . or Doctor Pepper. She liked Doctor Pepper. God only knows what was goin' on when I left. Mah hands was a-killin' me then, too. All strutted by the mis'ry. Not that she ever paid it no mind. Never said a thing. . . . R.D., turn that mear 'round so's I can look at mah rash."

The driver turned her reflection toward her.

"Bes' thing for arthritis is to iron it they say. It's the dry heat, you know." She held a moment in her words. "Don't you jus' hate t'have machines 'gainst your skin though?"

Several rows behind her, a young woman suddenly raised her head above the seat. Her hair was like cornsilk, parted on the side.

Down the aisle and across from her, two old country women were sharpening their speech. They crackled like little fires. Then another noise added to theirs; the girl with the light yellow hair was laughing at something they'd said. The two old ladies paused a moment, and the sound went out.

A man in work clothes and his young wife, who was near to child, sat behind me. They smelled of vinegar and earth. Her breasts were heavy with milk. They had a tow sack of pecans, and he would put two in his hand and crack one, and she would separate the nut from the shell.

The blonde girl's position never varied. She was taking a carriage. Its spokes broke the sun into a thousand pieces, and sent them reeling.

"How are you, Miss Della?" the driver asked her. He looked at his watch, which had a black face.

"I'm fine, thank you."

"Did you find that dress you was after?"

"I found it, but . . . prices are scandalous," she said.

The bus traveled through the landscape of my childhood—up through Arlington and Mason and Brownsville and Bells, where it started raining and the road smoked, and the wheels of the cars passing were all angry with water.

We pulled in at a truckstop not far out of Bells. I got down to use the restroom, but it was a sad place. A man dressed in a white uniform pushed another man in a wheelchair up to the urinal beside me, and put the brakes against the wheel. The crippled man was not old, but he was dressed in old man clothes. He had on glasses with one lens covered with black electrical tape, and though he talked, he did so in a voice you would have to listen to a long time to understand. He faintly resembled a marsupial, as if his body had been sinking for years into the place he sat, and his face was long with a kind of horse gentleness to it. His nurse unzipped him and propped him up from behind. It took a great deal of strength to accomplish this. The crippled man's head wobbled around until it came to look upon me. He drooled.

"Behave yourself, Nash," the nurse said.

I stood there and read the obscenities the philosophers had left behind on the wall. Before these two arrived I'd been thinking about the girl with the yellow hair. But now those thoughts had joined the countless other things I could no longer find in my life. And I have a terrible fear of turning a corner some day and finding them all accumulated in a pile I could never get around.

I looked at the girl when I returned to the bus. She wore a long white dress and boots made of blue suede. In her hand she twirled a red leaf with yellow borders.

The country people got on and got off; young and old changed seats— dressed in their dungarees and buckles, in their skirts where the colors only whispered. They began to blend into one another, and I heard a voice on a dream telephone. I rode the conversation down a long thin mirror on a highway made of heat. There was a whistle moaning on the horizon, and a black train whose smoke made the uncountable doves.

Out of the dark center of the doves stepped a clown. He was a tremendously fat clown with the skinny face of a mouse, and he wore a big striped bowtie. The clown began taking off his clothes. Under every layer of clothes there was another. Under each hat, another hat appeared. The clown undressed until he was quite thin. He seemed to be starving. And I noticed now that, as the clown undressed, he begged for food.

I pulled my pockets inside out and shrugged and gave the clown a little smile, but he would not accept it. He undressed until he was down to his skin. Even the bowtie came alive and flew away like a moth, and the noise of its wings made shapes in my hearing:

"He's talkin' to you."

"Hm?"

"He's talkin' to you," the blonde girl said. She had her hand on my shoulder and was shaking me a little. She nodded toward the driver, and, as I looked at him, he beckoned.

He thought he knew me, but I told him he was mistaken.

"No. It was you," he said. "You couldn't a been mor'n nine or ten . . . you'd just buried something. Something small. An' you marked the grave with a popsicle cross."

Afterwards then, she stayed sitting by me. I smelled bad. She wore perfume. She had the kind of face that, when looked at closely, changes its angles. Her eyes were hazel. Up close too, she was older; she wasn't any schoolgirl, yet even her time lines were somehow strategic, so that she was declining in an attractive way. I decided that she was probably over 30, which was ancient to me then. And though she tried to be young and easy, there was in her manner a polite Southern distance.

"Why you goin' to Paris for?"

I thought for a moment of telling her the truth, that I was thinking very seriously about killing my father, that this was what he deserved. But I knew saying it aloud would make it sound like a fool's errand. And I didn't think she'd take it well. She looked like a sensitive type.

"I'm passing through," I said.

I felt in my pocket for my sister's letter. It rained the day it arrived—a slow, Mexican rain with the sun still shining. I sat across from my hotel, in the park where the black squirrels lived. When I opened the envelope I tore my name, and the words bled in the rain.

"It's just as well . . . you'd be outa place. In Paris they might call you names." She crossed her legs. From her knee down was a brace; no muscle on the bone;

the shank of her leg slightly warped.

"What's the matter?" she said.

I lifted the dress off her leg a little, but she stopped me.

"You're certainly bold," she said. "I don't even know you."

She looked past me to herself in the window when she spoke.

I gave her my name which she put in her mouth.

"Bogan Cordele . . . Bogan Cordele," she said, "the sugar trees are lovely now." She gave me the red leaf with yellow borders.

"That's an old name here," she said. "Cordeles own popcorn land. . . ."

Then I was in an autumn field, shoulder high in the bowing stalks. My father, whose land this was as far as the eye could gather, stood to my right, and Bukka loaded his guns. Behind us were yellow maples. The horses had cobs in their mouths and chewed nervously. I was young and a hero among the fallen. The field was red. There was so much dove death around us, the day took a wrong turn. I felt this inside, and I saw it in the eyes of the horses.

"Your eyes just now," she said, "looked like they were dreaming."

The bus stopped at a light pole and green bench. A muscular young man with sad hair and sunburned arms got on. He had a transistor radio that sang sarcastically. The driver said to him:

"Hey Ballard."

"Hey," he said, and his back and head sank down a seat.

Out the window there was a rooster that had been struck by a car. Its lower body was crushed flat to the shoulder of the road, but the bird was alive; its head was up, and it looked around and blinked thoughtfully. A little black boy walked past with aluminum cans bent around his shoes. He clanked down the asphalt. The rooster was white with a red comb.

The bus started up, and in the window, autumn crossed my face. The air had begun to grain. Some leaves fell down the wind. I knew if I caught one before it touched the ground, I would have a good dream. But something else entered my reflection—as if the mirrors had run out of my shape—there in the window was an expression of my father's that I particularly disliked.

I felt the revolver, hard in the boot against my skin. I remembered how I'd broken it down into its blue parts and washed it in oil; and as I reassembled it, how it had begun to fit my purpose.

The girl had been looking me over, and her eyes did not always know where to end.

"Why you wear your hair so long for?"

When I didn't answer, her smile stumbled and fell.

I watched the driver. He was a very careful driver. If he hit a cat, I thought, he'd run over it nine times. But he enjoyed what he was doing; he had made a game of it. He was playing auto chess in the black and red forest.

Now as he reversed lanes, and crossed the center, time stood in two. I am by a still pond in one of the distant years. In front of me tower stark factory buildings with CORDELE MATCH printed on them. I am young and just beginning to know the lie of my name. Something different hinged on this moment; after it, I would start my long journey into Nigger and the empire of my muscles.

I came here often to listen to the frogs. There were thousands of them. I found their songs soothing, while the voices of men were all decibels and anguish. They were strange, beautiful creatures—blue and stunted by the sulfur that emptied into the water. And I understood from a story I'd been told, they would all one day be princes. Glancing down, I discovered the red frog with one great eye in the center of its back. And ever after my mind was of two colors.

"I didn't mean to be cross."

"I'm sorry, too," she said. "It must be the moon. I haven't been myself . . . here I've gone and interrupted your privacy."

"Tonight will make hunter's moon."

"Yes," she said. "I've never seen the winter quite so late. I would have to call this Indian summer."

Beneath her rudeness there was a certain charm. And something sexual—something that said, Would you take my hand into the night? I hurried through this thought toward my destination, though the countryside no longer seemed to move.

"Mr. Slade's the driver," she was saying. "I've known him since I can remember. He runs the bus for people along this road. They go down the road apiece and git off. Some of 'em go into Memphis shopping. That boy there, Ballard . . . he operates the forklift at the lumber yard in Paris. His brother Narvel (she whispered) is the one's been charged with sexual 'salt . . . did you hear 'bout it?"

Now when I turned I discovered my reflection and shadow in the seat behind us. My shadow began to imitate struggles that darken the grace of the evening. My image snored in the voices of the dead.

I had always taken my shadow to be the past; it walked behind me without question. My reflection I took for the future; in it there is little resemblance to who I am, only what I will become. Just recently it had fashioned a key made of glass and escaped from the mirrors. A wretched creature, it has taken to lounging on park benches, and this is not the first time I have caught it napping under newspapers stained by the weather.

All told, this dream had seven children. They began to crowd the bus, joked among themselves, speculated on the secrets they had witnessed. One of them was kind enough to tell me I was sleeping.

This same one took the leaf and returned it to Della. When Della touched it, the leaf became a fan, and she opened it. The fan was painted with a scene: A lady there looked out on autumn, her face half-covered by a veil embroidered with white flowers; her hair was long and wheat red; her expression had forgotten history, committed a crime, was raised by animals; the day she looked out on did not move; it was brittle and glazed with the color yellow; she wore a black dress long out of style and called to someone beyond the world.

Now as Della fanned herself with this scene, the voices and laughter of the children muted, and the bus was infected with silence. It blew every motion to sleep. And the woman on the fan began to unbraid her hair, and comb it with the skeleton of a fish.

A moth flew out of her sleeve. Its wings were not in time, and it circled into the mirror of the bus. The glass broke perfectly, regained its appearance, and the moth sat in a small world, with the rumor that all was not well burning in its eyes.

This turned everything around. The girl beside me had the face of a cornflower. We talked seven miles like children. She said I could be the king of her body, though I must rule in a deep fit of hallucination. And out of the fan an arm reached down, and a hand touched me.

I began to hear the rain, the tires record the pulse of the highway, and I awoke. Della slept against my shoulder, with her hand on the pocket of my jeans. Her mouth moved silently on my linen shirt; my cock was hard and took breaths of blood.

She moved, and her hand sucked on me; but when I looked over, her eyes were still closed. It disarmed me completely, I'll tell you that.

And when I tried to touch her, she wouldn't at first allow this—though she parted the folds of her dress until I could see the darkness under it.

It was all so insane; during it, I noticed my father laughing hysterically in the window.

The world outside began to slow, as the bus backed down its gears, and the rain tired, and the afternoon stopped near a barn where a lantern hung. A man stood in a halo. His shoulders were broad; they cut the light in two. He came into the bus and shook off the outside, an old black man in a raincoat and hood. He wore dark glasses and had a white cane. The driver called him King Arthur, and King Arthur walked by him without paying.

"Arthur," the driver said. "Arthur," he said, and swore under his breath. But King Arthur was blind in the ears as well, and kept walking.

"Come next time I ain't stoppin', Arthur. This bus run on diesel and ile. . . ."

As King Arthur shambled down the hall of the bus, the rain frogs in the forest sang above the engine and the voice of the driver, and a single light broke through the fog in the south, came even with the bus, roared slowly by: two insect faces echoed down the windows.

"You're beholden to me, Arthur. Don't come 'round in the mornin' . . . you bes' stay t'home now on . . . tell ole Millie you ain't gone be aroun'. Tell Charlie Mae, too. . . ."

King Arthur followed his cane.

"Ballard," the driver said, "stop him. . . ."

The boy with the sad hair tugged on King Arthur's sleeve and turned him. He walked him back to the driver. King Arthur stood before the driver and fished in the pocket of the raincoat. He took a canning jar from the pocket. The jar was full of dark, rust-colored preserves, sealed at the top with paraffin. He held it out in front of him. The driver stared at the jar.

"Where am?" King Arthur said.

"I got a whole shelf a pear preserves, Arthur. I don't need no more preserves."

"Where am?"

The driver glowered at him, shook his head in exasperation, took the jar.

"Gone sit down," he said, but King Arthur had turned already. He stalked on to the last row where the seat crossed the length of the bus, sat, and thumped his cane impatiently . . . until once again the bus climbed through its gears down the road.

The fog was serried now, like driving through cotton; the headlights were absorbed by it.

There was Della and me, Ballard, the driver, King Arthur; no one said a word. After awhile, Della yawned and opened her eyes. It was all make believe; she was careful not to look in my direction.

I felt somewhat puzzled, but I knew what was real. I could still smell her on my fingers. She, in the meantime, appeared to have just caught herself coming downstairs with a beast. She combed her hair and a long silence passed, behind which she once more composed her purity—a white flower suspended in God.

I finally mumbled some foolishness, all but unintelligible, even I couldn't quite hear it, like water talking downstream. She didn't hear me, or didn't understand it, or she didn't want to. She stared out the window, even though there was nothing left to see but the cloud we drove through.

The motor of the bus coughed, backfired; the driver downshifted, and turned the wheel. The bus came to a stop on the shoulder of the road, under a county highway bridge. A red flare burned a circle in the fog.

Two figures passed through the lights. Ballard sat upright and cocked his head. The driver cranked the doors open, and though he talked, his voice suddenly grew much smaller. As the doors yawed, a kind of skull with a blue tooth entered, and out in front of it was a Luger.

The gun went off, through the roof, and the old man fell to the floor and began to curl up; he tried to make himself so small death could not find him.

The other man came onto the bus, holding a small-bore pistol.

"Rex!" he shouted.

"I didn't hurt him, Jack," Rex said. "Lest I scared him to death."

They walked down the aisle. The one named Rex looked at Della, and the look burned her down. Then he turned to me and scowled.

"I seen this joker somewheres," he said.

"He ain't the one," Jack said. He turned his head like a mantis and looked Ballard up and down.

"What's your name?"

Ballard's mouth faltered and betrayed the mood of his face, which suddenly came undone altogether. His breath somersaulted a couple times then.

Rex and Jack turned to each other and talked low. I could hear their voices, yet I could not shape them to my advantage.

I had the revolver in the well of my boot, but their guns followed every movement.

"What's with the nigger?" Jack said.

King Arthur was thumping his cane.

"Your name Caufield?" Rex said to Ballard. "You be the brother of Narvel Caufield? Say your name," he said.

Ballard only shuddered.

"Stop thumpin' the cane, old man. . . ."

"He can't hear you."

"Who axt you?" Jack said. "Look . . . I got nothin' agin you, but you open your mouth one more time. . . ."

Then he said to Rex, "C'mere an' watch this lug."

He put the gun to Ballard's temple. "Drop them trousers," he said.

When the boy did not obey, he slapped him twice with the pistol; blood threaded down from Ballard's eye; he spit out a tooth.

"Stand up," he said. He undid Ballard's buckle; the trousers fell and bunched around his knees. "Turn around." Then he said to Rex, "Go on."

Rex lifted the hair from off the back of Ballard's neck and twined it in a ring around his finger, bent him down by it.

"How you like bein' a little girl?" Jack said bitterly. He held the pistol to Ballard's head again. "You needn't answer me your name . . . the likeness is strong. You take a message to your brother, hear? He brung shame on a good person . . . tell him she is my sister . . . mine! Tell it to him in hell," he said, and he pulled the trigger. The hammer clicked. And again, and nothing happened.

But the third time, in his temple it spoke a lead prayer.

Ballard staggered forward in the aisle. He walked downward to the floor and spilled his life there.

Their eyes were locked on this and I drew my .38. Jack turned and started a word, but a bullet shattered his voice. I fired till the gun was empty.

My hearing rang, cold and dim. My face moved in the windows, black with powder. Della crawled along the aisle, crawled under a seat like a snake. In my confusion, I turned and faced King Arthur. His head swung from side to side, violently smelling the air. My voice was far away and muffled, as though it came from another time. I was talking to him. I was telling him everything . . . but he only thumped his cane.

It was what woke me again.

The King of Everything

The back of El Rey de Todos bar in Melchor, Guatemala, opens onto a courtyard. There are seven rooms built into the ochre and blue walls of the courtyard, and a number of tables and chairs sitting around the enclosed area under thatch umbrellas. Each room has a wooden door and a slatted window. If a room is occupied at the time, the girl leaves her shoes outside the door. The rooms that aren't occupied have a dimestore lock on them. Each girl has a key. They make a big deal out of having these. They like to slap them down on the table in front of you while they light their cigarettes. One of the doors, Shameface noted, had two pairs of shoes outside it. Noise came from that room, laughter. "They're doin' some stunt fuckin' in there," he said to Harlan across the table. Harlan Green turned his head and stared at the door. His eyes were so red they appeared to be all but on fire. They were both quite drunk at this particular moment—what was it? about 4:00 in the afternoon now—and anyone watching could tell from their sodden behavior the day was building toward something truly wrong and perverse.

They were an unlikely pair. Shameface went 5'9" and two-forty-nine. He had a big, shaggy head and a graying Palestinian beard that didn't mask his pockmarked features. He had a gin nose which sat like an ornament upon his face. Whether out of pride or humor, no one knew, he claimed to be the ugliest white man in the Cayo valley. He was probably correct in this assessment. Nobody ever asked what he did for money. He told people he had retired, though he wasn't but forty-two years old. The prime of life, as he put it. He had on shapeless, all but colorless Bermuda shorts, a sleeveless T-shirt, a black ball cap, and big black rubber boots. See there's a saltwater crab in Belize coastal waters that's so nasty looking it is called Shameface, and this was his namesake. All his friends started calling him that years ago, though, to be honest, he doesn't have but about three-four friends. They thought it comical at the time. He doesn't always think so, even now, just depends on his frame of mind, but there's little to do about it at this late date—the name took.

Harlan Green was tall, gaunt, a slightly stoop-shouldered Texan, with a sandy, long handlebar mustache, a bootcamp haircut with a receding hairline. His right eye was always about half closed and his left abnormally open as if it'd just been totally surprised recently. Even sitting inanimate as he was now, he looked somewhat berserk. It was a face that belonged on a wanted poster about a hundred years ago, except for his gold earring maybe. And though he was long and skinny, he had a little potbelly that poked through his shirt where a button was missing. He was a mechanic up at Johnny Roberson's lumber yard; transmission fluid decorated his shirt and jeans. At the moment he was on vacation and fixing to go back to Houston soon for Christmas. He'd been at it for three days and nights just about, and for all that, he seemed fairly lucid. Shameface had been drinking for twelve hours, and he was a mess. In that time they'd been to three whorehouses in Belize and four in Guatemala. They thought it was Saturday, but neither of them was sure. And yet, such was their present environment, they fit in barely noticed. Melchor being such a raffish town.

The scene in the courtyard is constantly changing, but just to frame that for a moment, it looks like so: The boys are sitting at a thatched table nearly in the middle of the floor. The door closest to them is five feet away. The threesome in there is still having at it. At the northern-most table, up by the bar, three Guatemalans are playing cards. There's money on the table—green quetzals, the Guatemalan dollar. One of them has a black eye-patch, one a little straw hat with the brim pushed up in the front; the third one is younger than these two and has most of the money in front of him. They are oblivious to the distractions around them. At another table, a Mayan sits alone fanning the pages of a paperback novel with one hand. He's dressed like a cowboy. He holds the book up by his left ear; he has his elbow on the table; he fans the pages from time to time like he's listening to what the book has to tell him. There's another fella in the courtyard who doesn't sit down, or when he does, it's not for long. Maybe ten years ago he'd been handsome. Maybe it was last year. A man can fall to ruin quickly in the tropics. Now his face is completely dissolute. He keeps shifting around the place, looking in the windows now and then of the rooms where the wooden louvers are open enough to see. His features are more Spanish than anyone else there. The girls call him something like Stagedoor Johnny. At another table, two whores sit. One is playing solitaire, while the other follows the game closely, making suggestions sometimes on a play. It's their time of the month. An older American lounges at another table. He'd just finished and is red in the face and satisfied. There's a drink in front of him which he ignores. He stares off, sucking his teeth obscenely like a large upright fish. Just by the way he's dressed, he's probably the only one in the place with real money, and these girls can be had for the equivalent of $7.50 American. He's sitting pretty. The rest of these guys, they only put on shoes when they come to town. A skinny old lady sweeps the floor with a broom made of palmetto leaves. She runs the place, though she hardly looks the part. She's her own best customer on the rum. The girls come and go in their shiny, brightly colored dresses that are supposed to look like satin. There's several taxi drivers from Cayo that Shameface knew who had brought tourists over the border to do some shopping. Two young Mennonites from Spanish Lookout are drinking rum and coke. It would be hard to place them as Mennonites. The Mennonites from Spanish Lookout are thoroughly modern and look just like American rednecks. They're speaking German with a kind of Creole lilt to it. Next to them is a water spigot with a short hose on it and a pigtail bucket underneath. The less bashful of the girls, if they are in a hurry say, will squat there, hike up their skirt or towel, and wash it off in broad daylight. The others take a pitcher to it, then return with the pitcher to the room. All of this is accompanied by dolorous Spanish music drifting out from the bar, and the laughter of drunks.

The boys ordered another round. They were drinking Gallo beer mixed with tomato juice. They'd been drinking rum earlier, but they wanted to be alert once it got dark. They'd needed a restorative a short time earlier and had purchased some speed at one of the local pharmacies. It was starting to work. Shameface drank some of his beer out of the bottle, opened the little tomato juice can and poured it into the beer. He shifted his toothpick around from one corner of his mouth to the other.

"Tell it to me again, Harlan," he said. "Say it slower this time, and try to let it make sense."

Well, Harlan Green had come knocking on Shameface's door at 3:30 the previous night. He was standing out there in a storm soaking wet, said he had to talk, asked if he could bring his pipe in with him. His pipe turned out to be an empty Schlitz beer can.

"Smoke?" he asked

"No," Shameface said, "I wouldn't want to do that."

"Mind if I do?"

"No, hell, go on ahead. Knock yourself out."

Shameface watched him smoke the rocks out of his beer can pipe.

"Harlan," he said, "what's that shit do for you?"

"Well, it gets you higher'n a bat, then pretty soon it drops you just that fast . . . and afterwards it's like, Hey, what the fuck is my name?"

"How long you been in Belize now?"

"Goin' on three years."

"I think you been here too long," Shameface said.

But he heard him out. Harlan talked until dawn. Around first light it started raining again. It'd been raining since November 27th, and here it was almost Christmas. Then Harlan went out to the porch and fell asleep on the hammock for a couple hours. He'd rambled a wild tale, little of which made any sense. Toward the end there he was starting to turn his words around, talking backwards. Shameface couldn't tell what he was saying.

Now in El Rey de Todos bar—this means The King of Everything or The King of It All—he told it again:

"Well, I saw a woman bathing down there by the river. She was blonde. When I went towards her, I was so damn high, I couldn't seem to get to her. I got lost down there in the dark. After awhile I fell asleep. I woke up in a graveyard. One a them little ones they got around here, four, five crypts, painted in pastel colors—"

"She was takin' a bath," Shameface interrupted, "but you said before, she had on a robe."

"Yeah, she did . . . a white, flimsy sort of robe. An' she was bathin' or goin' to anyways . . . I tell you, I'm not sure on the particulars. You think we're fucked up now, but . . . last night, man, I was gone."

"Okay, go on . . . you seen her there . . . then what?"

"I seen her, and . . . then she showed me her tits. That's about it. Then I got lost."

"Was she pretty?"

"I didn't get a good look at her face. Maybe she was crying or something. Like her face was averted. But that body,"—he made motions with his hands, rolled his head around, gave Shameface a big downward grin, as if the beauty involved therein was unconveyable, and yet—"that body was *it,* buddy."

And he'd told the story enough times now in the past twelve hours without once laughing out loud that Shameface had got his interest up.

Besides, what had it been now? 23-24 straight days of rain in Cayo. He'd been drinking himself insensible every other day during that period. On the off day he'd recover. There was absolutely nothing else to do but get drunk during the day and listen to the dogs bark at night. Very rarely did it even thunder or lightning, just the steady business of raining. So anything out of the ordinary was welcome relief, even this improbable quest they were on now.

Just then Lourdes came and sat beside him, bless her heart. Lourdes was a Creole girl from San Ignacio who'd worked for years at Caracol, the whorehouse out at Georgeville. Then her mother died, and her grandmother became responsible for her. Granny didn't mind in the least that she worked at a whorehouse, but she was against Lourdes' drinking habits and told her finally if she didn't stop getting dead drunk every night, she'd make her quit her job and enter a convent. And she wanted it stopped in a timely fashion. Lourdes had skipped the country on that one and come over to work in Guatemala.

Her and Shameface were old buddies, been that way since she was seventeen, which was a couple hard years ago. She had a crush on him that wouldn't quit. That was something nobody could figure, not even him—that ugly as he was, that tell-tale face, belly hanging over his belt and all, a certain section of the ladies just ate it up, hanging around with this big ole nasty fucker. Maybe it made them feel pretty in comparison.

But much as Lourdes cared for him, she harbored an equal dislike of Harlan Green. Nobody knew exactly why, except he did have a bad habit of mispronouncing her name. He called her Lard Ass. And even though the name was appropriate—she was a generous portion, like somebody'd inflated her with a bicycle pump actually—it was hardly tasteful.

She sat there smiling at Shameface. Her mahogany skin was shining. She had her hair in jheri curls, wore a plum-colored sarong, dangling zebra earrings, which closely resembled bass lures Shameface once used in his younger days in Tampa. He nodded to her. Harlan started to say something but didn't get a chance.

"Fock you," Lourdes growled. "Don' vex me, mahn."

On the way over to Melchor in Harlan's pickup, they'd heard on the British Armed Forces Radio broadcast that a man near London had been arrested for having indecent relations with a dolphin. Some people'd been out sightseeing in a boat, and they'd spotted the two of them in the water carrying on. That'd been hours ago they'd heard this, but out of the blue now, Shameface commented on it:

"I guess it was better'n get caught with a damn mullet," he said.

Harlan tied into what he was talking about, and the two of them got to laughing. Lourdes was a little put out, not getting the joke.

"Shame," she said, "you want to juke?"

"Maybe later," he said.

She smiled at him and went on about her duties.

Shameface went to the urinal to take a leak. He was looking over the fields that led down to the Mopan River. There was a flock of sheep in the field closest to the bar. He saw this through the wrought iron bars on the window opening—they were made into the shape of hearts. He had to hold his breath because of the urinal stink. If you stood over toward the drain, you'd piss on your foot. It was one of those. He gave his pipe a knock or two and walked up toward the bar. He passed Harlan at the table, who had one of the girls in his lap—a squat Indian with a wide mouth. She had on an electric blue dress. He glanced at her and thought about toads just briefly. He looked over the girls in the bar. A couple big Salvadoran brutes, more Guatemalans, half wild, surly. A Honduran who dressed differently than the rest; she'd been watching American TV, perhaps. She was lively but had some disconcerting plague marks on her face. Well, this was the crux of the matter: They'd been to seven whorehouses now in one day and hadn't yet come across a pretty woman.

Four Guatemalan soldiers were sitting at the bar. They were lean, and smart in their olive uniforms, their Israeli machine pistols. They all looked to be about 17. They were drinking beer and flirting with a barmaid.

Shameface stood there looking out the doorway onto the white mud streets of Melchor. The biggest crowd in town was down the way in front of the TV store. They were watching TV from the street. He was staring at the sky, all doom and iron—looked like God's beard and it was going to rain again surely, it didn't know how stop anymore—when a kid came walking a pig by. It was the biggest pig he could remember seeing, maybe 350-400 pounds. The kid had a switch in his hand, but he didn't seem to need it. It was like he was out walking the dog. They stopped at the door, and the kid looked around the bar. Shameface thought for awhile maybe the pig was going to come in—a specialty item!

The speed was going now. He was hard up against it. His mind felt like it was highballing into a big city.

"Let me ask you this, Harlan," he said once he returned to the courtyard and sat down at the table (Shameface's eyes were starting to glitter in the dusk), "that one you had setting on your lap . . . did she do anything for you? Say in comparison to the blonde last night?"

"Not even close," Harlan replied. "Hell, I don't even like to fuck these whores," he went on, "I jus' likes to fight 'em. . . ."

Right here, Shameface realized later, he should have been paying more attention to what was said, but at the time, he just studied Harlan, nodded. Harlan's face looked like it had caught a few too many punches somewhere back along the line. When he got really wasted, it just went slack. Sort of fell to pieces on him. That's how it looked now, Shameface realized. He was gone. Grinding his teeth.

"You startin' to come on line, ain't you boy?"

Then here comes the Indian girl back, and she's got another one with her. They both looked alike. This one's dress was emerald green.

"They sisters," Harlan said. They both slapped their keys on the table. Harlan raised his eyebrows. His left eye about to pop out of his head, he commented: "On second thought. . . ." He kicked his heavy motorcycle boots together to knock some of the mud off them, picked up both keys, winked at Shameface, and the three of them moved off to a room directly to the side of the table.

Shameface was sitting alone, seemingly deep in thought—though, actually his thoughts weren't exactly long journeys from start to finish at the moment. A little plate of fried meat and peppers had been delivered to the table. Compliments of Lourdes no doubt. The meat was gray. Harlan's cigarettes and matches were sitting beside it. The matchbook said *Detengamos El Colera.* Damn Harlan. He liked Harlan alright, but the boy, when he tied his shoe, he had his other shoe tied to it . . . you know what I mean? he asked his mind. This whole business about the blonde was probably nonsense. There were two red doves in the big orange tree overhanging the courtyard. A green hummingbird in the coral vine. He ordered another drink. Outside the walls, occasionally a horse would nicker or a lamb bleat, and the bed Harlan and the two girls occupied would seem to squeal in reply.

Then of all things, a young deer came wandering into the courtyard. The old lady who ran the place sent one of the girls away, and shortly she came back with a bottle of milk. It was just like a baby bottle, but bigger. The old lady held the bottle up, and the deer really had at it. Afterwards, it went over and checked out the dogfood bowl, see if there was anything in there. Then it walked around looking at the people. It came up to Shameface, looked him over, sniffed his beer and moved on.

Shameface thought: I wonder if it likes gray meat?

"That's the only deer I ever met in a bar," Shameface commented to the old lady. "I think," he added. But she didn't understand English anyway, so what the hell. He was sort of taken with the gentleness of the scene, which, however, didn't prevent him from recalling several venison dishes he'd savored over the years. It was a nice quiet moment in the courtyard, all of which was shattered not even a minute later by screaming in Harlan's room.

The door burst open and Harlan and one of the girls rolled buck naked onto the floor. He had the girl in a headlock. The second sister jumped on; pretty soon Harlan had each one in a headlock. He's got a head under each arm. He's saying, "Do you give? Say 'Uncle' goddamn it!" Then here come Lourdes in a dead trot from the bar, goes airborne about three feet from the pile and does a bellyflop square on Harlan's back. Flattened him like roadkill.

Awhile later they were making their way toward the river.

Harlan said, "Quit laughing . . . damn it. She jus' knocked the wind out a me is all."

"She knocked you out, jack."

Harlan looked back toward the bar, even though he couldn't see it anymore.

"Lord, I jus' love mean women." He stopped, turned to the side and commenced to do a little projectile vomiting.

Shameface watched him as he tried to clean himself up with one of them rags most people check their oil with.

"Harlan," he said, "you got any family . . . I mean like . . . human family?"

"Sure, I got family. I got a brother, anyway . . . his name's Pink."

"Pink?" Shameface said. "So his name's Pink Green?"

"Yeah, why?" Harlan said.

Then they were following a path along the river. It was dark, but you could see, too. It was frog holler and crickets like little sawmills and the river rush—you'd hear it all and then you wouldn't. Harlan commented, "I tell you what, last night I had a hell of a time gettin' through them sheep. I kept steppin' on 'em. It was rainin'. You couldn't see shit. . . . I wouldn't doubt the old lady puts high heels on them babies late at night. The good lookin' ones anyway."

"How'd you happen to get out here in the first place?"

"I don't recall exactly. I think maybe I was lookin' for my truck."

"Harlan, not to put too fine a point on it, but . . . what would the truck be doin' out here?"

"You got me, bud," he said.

"There's the graveyard." Harlan pointed it out on a rise. The crypts were blue and pink and white. There were maybe six crosses.

"But the girl was farther up. Damn . . . I don't know. This is exactly how I got last night. Like my direction was all gone to hell."

"You think maybe she was a ghost, Harlan?" It was a little foggy right where they were and real stony looking.

"Jesus, I hope not. I thought she was a tourist."

Shameface looked around. He marked his way. There were lights from the shops across the river. He could see the border crossing there.

"There . . . look!" Harlan whispered.

He pointed to a place where the river bent inward, toward some large white rocks along the bank.

"That's it," he said. "Right there. Just stood there she was."

Shameface saw it then. They were 20-25 yards away, but there was definitely something yellow in his view. Like a big dishevelled head of yellow hair amongst the tree branches.

Harlan saw it then, too. It was back off the river some, next to the giant trunk of a cotton tree whose white bark seemed to catch what light there was to have.

"She ain't movin'," Shameface said. "She watchin' us?"

Harlan was skeptical.

"I don't know," he said. "I don't know what the hell that is. It ain't the same. . . ."

Shameface wasn't listening. He said, "We gone be the King of Everything, man."

Well the boys were standing with their heads pointed out in front of them like a couple bird dogs, Shameface holding his breath even, but then all of a sudden Harlan just let it loose.

"Aw hell, Shame," he said, and he started ambling over to the yellow place and the giant cotton tree. "That ain't nothin' but damn bananas."

And sure enough, that's what it was, a big long bunch of apple bananas somebody'd cut the stalk of and hung up to ripen. They were yellow ripe, some of the little thumb-sized fruit already starting to break off.

Harlan lit a cigarette.

Shameface just stared. It was almost like he was in shock.

"She sure was a whole lot fancier lookin' last night," Harlan commented.

Then he turned philosophical.

"How old are you now, Shame?" he asked.

Shameface didn't move. He seemed dumbstruck, but he answered in a low, measured voice: "I'm 42."

"Does it bother you gettin' older?"

"Yeah, it does, Harlan." The only thing that moved was his mouth.

"What bothers you most about it?"

"I think death, probably," he said.

"I'm gettin' older," Harlan said. "Gettin' too old to be carrying on like this. I can't do it any more, but I keep tryin' . . . ."

Shameface looked down at his hands. They looked like they held an invisible jar. He was shaking. He turned and stared at Harlan's neck.

Harlan was drawing on his cigarette. The first raindrops struck then and put it out. Shameface's head dropped back, he looked directly up, just let the rain beat on him, but it didn't help.

The huge cotton tree was five feet away from them. Harlan was about to make his next sage observation when Shameface dropped his shoulders and ran directly into the tree trunk head first. He flew backward past Harlan so fast, Harlan had to snap his head to watch it, so severely had Shameface been rejected by the wood. He came up grinning, and did it again. He had more of a headstart this time, but slightly less gumption, and the collision stopped him dead in his tracks. He slid down to the ground and sat there blinking like a goat.

A third assault would be ill-advised, perhaps, and anyway, he'd regained his senses.

Harlan knelt beside him.

"Damn, son," he said.

"Get me to Lourdes," Shameface said. "Find me a sheep, I don't give a goddamn, it's gettin' late."

Just then some night bird out there cried like a widow. And the best part of the story ended on that note.

Forgetting How to Laugh

I recall now the seasons leading to that summer. The winding down of color from the trees that autumn. Time moved like maple syrup then. The killing frost. And how we marked the 1st of winter one day in early November when we had to force the dog outside because he took up too much of the heater. And the winter itself, as each one previous, that before it was over my very thoughts would turn to snow. At the end of March, spring came unexpectedly one afternoon. I walked home from school, drunk on the warm light. Then summer vacation. It was the summer of 1952 in northern Ohio. The sky was hot and gray. The Five and Dime sold painted turtles. I kept them in a wash tub with crawfish and tadpoles from the creek. In the heat of the afternoons, my sister and I would have to stay indoors and rest, for our parents were afraid of us getting polio. I was eight years old. This is how things had always been. Nothing had ever broken them.

My sister was so much older than me that summer I just couldn't hardly stand her anymore. In June she got to be sixteen. Uncle Grant taught her how to drive. Aunt Jim would ride along with them, just to get out. Daddy, he didn't want any part of it. She had memorized the book of rules and could drive around on the streets well enough, but parallel parking was something beyond her. We had a four-door Pontiac then that stretched from about here to there. It may have been one of the longest cars ever manufactured in the world. And though she practiced parking every day between two poles outside the bowling alley, that part of the test had her worried to the point of distraction.

I wasn't pleased that Mom had to take me along with them that morning to the courthouse. I had more important things to do. Then a policeman, about bigger'n all three of us put together, made us stay behind while he took my sister for her driving test. My sister tried to smile as he led her away, but her face didn't exactly move.

She tried to chat with the po-lice some, but he wasn't having any of it; and I could, knowing her so well, tell right then that she'd come undone, though she moved along beside him with what I guess she thought was pure nonchalance.

But then she got right next to that four-door sedan, and damn if she didn't open the back door of it and get in. She calmly sat down in the back seat and reached up to take hold of the streering wheel, though it wasn't there at all, of course. She told me many years later that she had commented to herself just then, "Now where in hell'd that go?"

The policeman, in the meantime, had climbed into the shotgun seat and looked over to where my sister should have been, then looked back. Well, it come into my sister to just slide on out of there, that maybe nobody'd notice too much. But she happened to turn around when she was closing the door, and Mom and I were in the background there doubled up. We laughed until we hurt, and I couldn't stop it the rest of the day.

But it wasn't even a week later to that day when the summer, and all it meant to me, came to an end.

We had only known polio as a name. Then the neighborhood started dropping with it all at once. Nancy Aldolfer got it first. I had used to play with her, and it made a big impression on me that they brought an ambulance for her in the middle of the afternoon. She was never to come back. But by that night, it took me, too. It took me like the changing of the seasons, only in an evil way.

Then I was in a bed at Children's Hospital in Akron, and my parents were looking at me so strangely I thought almost that I had done something wrong. But it didn't really affect me so much, because I was about sick as three hundred dollars. Or say it's one night sometime later—when I went to sleep there were four of us in the room, but come the morning I was in there alone. And the nurse told me finally it's on account they were perfect children, and if a child is perfect, the faeries would come and take him. And that marked the last time I ever thought to be perfect in my life.

And the morning after that, when I woke up, they'd put me under the knife sometime before, made a cut on my throat, what they called a tracheotomy, and I had tubes in my nose. That's how they fed me for the next month, was through them tubes. I got so I would look in magazines and cut out pictures of food. I would put them in a scrapbook, and for the next month I collected scrapbooks of pictures of food. But even when they let me go home, I still couldn't swallow.

I had bulbar polio. Just several years ago, I found out the mortality rate for this type of polio was 99%. But I made it. And I was one of the lucky ones. You can go to northern Ohio tomorrow and meet some of the kids I grew up with, and see men and women whose arms and legs are useless and twisted unnaturally. All I came out of it was that I forgot how to laugh. I recall how I used to do it when I was little. I could laugh, I'll tell you. Ask my sister if you want.

But when I try to do it now, it ain't nowhere the same. Can you imagine it? Something so strong that for the rest of your life you can't remember how to laugh?

The Biggest Rat In The World

The Marines had a checkpoint at the wooden bridge where it crossed the river. NVA mortar teams periodically shelled the bridge. It was no more than a collection of patchwork, say as if the carpenters who built it were somewhat mad, and when a tank or self-propelled artillery piece crossed it, you had a tendency to close one eye and wag your head.

The dirt road was called Route 9. It ran roughly parallel to the DMZ, over from Dong Ha to Cam Lo to Camp Carroll, crossed the bridge here and started climbing to the Rock Pile, Khe Sanh. The road was red from the color of the earth. It ran west from this checkpoint through a long, narrow valley that was planted with rice. The rice shoots were bright green now, and the valley and the blue green mountains that rolled down to it looked delicate and old like painted china.

The Marines had bunkers built into the hillside. It was noon. Helicopters chuffed overhead. Some of the men slept, and others filled sandbags or broke down their weapons in the shade.

I asked one of the grunts at the bridge how long ago the convoy had passed.

"Maybe an hour."

"I need to go on."

"I don't reckon," he said.

"I got a case of Cokes," I said. "You're welcome to some, if you want."

He turned his head and called, "Hey, Billy." And Billy came over.

"The man wants to go through."

They both had stubble beards. Their flak jackets and the uniform pants rolled up above their boots and they themselves were dusty red. Each man wore an earring. Billy looked at me and said, "I recall you."

"He is got some Cokes," the other one said.

Billy looked to the west, where rain clouds were building.

"The convoy get through alright?"

"By the sound of it," Billy said, "they caught some shit."

I leaned against the handrail of the bridge and looked down at the river. It was sullen, and red like the earth. A number of fish floated belly up in the current.

"Somebody up above's fishin' with dynamite," Billy explained.

The other grunt said, "You got them Cokes or was you jus' talkin'?" So we went over to the jeep.

"How'd you happen to miss the convoy?"

"I had to wait for the mail," I said. This was partially true. The mail came in late. But while I was there, I ran into a clerk from Headquarters I knew, and he had some shit. Then it took me about two hours to get back around to where I could drive the jeep again.

"Wait till the lieutenant gets out a here," Billy said. "Then you can go. That dude there talkin'."

"What's he doin' here?"

"You tell me," Billy said. "Best you not in a hurry anyway. Charlie'll be takin' a nap pretty soon. You smart to wait awhile . . . we'll take a couple of these Cokes apiece. Jus' to drink," he said.

I walked down to the river and skipped some stones on it. The mountains fell down abruptly to the river on the other side. Vines crossed in the air like acrobats on that side, and there was a tribe of monkeys down at the water's edge. It was maybe fifty meters across.

Around the swimming hole at various places there were five men. Two of them were spades who sat under a tree shooting craps. There was a thin, tow-headed kid wearing dark glasses that you couldn't see into. And up the way some, two others were leaning against a truck. It was a deuce-and-a-half truck, the water a foot deep on the tires, and the men leaning on it were speaking

Spanish—one of them new, his uniform still dark green, and the other a broad-shouldered Latin kid with a blade tattooed on his right arm. They had a bucket of soapy water on the running board, and rags, and one of the doors had dried suds on it.

I sat down by the spades to watch their game. They were drinking beer and offered me one. They kept it in the river, so it wasn't altogether warm as I was used to. I rested against the bank, and while I drank, watched the clouds gather overhead and breathed the damp smell of the rain that was coming. It hadn't rained for some time. It started coming down then, not too hard, and didn't last long. The sun kept shining while it rained.

I learned from the conversation that one of the spades was called Cricket and the other, bigger one, Lodi.

Didn't nobody around use their true names much. Everybody had a nickname he went by. Now these fellas had a good game going. They were playing for money, a lot of money, but up along the Z, when you got paid there wasn't nothing to buy, so it didn't mean too much.

The one called Cricket had a big gap between his front teeth, and a certain expression fixed on his face that I can't describe correctly, other than to say it looked like the sun was always in his eyes. Lodi had a round face and a busted nose, and he wore soft-gold bracelets on his wrists. He had two earrings in each ear. He had a necklace with a cross on it, along with his dog tags. He had on all kinds of jewelry, but he was so tough looking, you couldn't picture anybody talking funny about it.

"How 'bout sportin' them bones," he said to Cricket just then.

"Wait up nigger!" Cricket answered.

"You losin' touch wid da game, s'what you doin'."

They went back and forth like that.

The tow-headed kid came over. He was reading a letter.

He said, "Where you headed?"

"The Rock Pile."

"You Army?"

"Yeah. The 175's," I said. "The battery that come through here this mornin'."

"The self-propelled?" he said. "You know them shells are big'n I am." He talked like maybe he was from Kentucky or West Virginia or somewhere, and I felt comfortable speaking with him.

"We saw them hit Charlie at Cam Lo. They are nasty motherfuckers now, I mean."

"I ain't never seen 'em hit," I said.

He looked at me and shook his head a little, as if this had confirmed a suspicion he'd held for some time about the Artillery.

Then he went back to his letter. He saw me watching him read and said:

"It's from my folks. We farmers," he said. He read some more. "Daddy says hog prices was good . . . an' that helped tote him through the winter."

Lodi threw the dice then, and they came up double aught. Didn't nobody say "snake eyes."

Cricket leaned an ear toward the dice and spoke to them:

"Wha'd you say?"

And it seemed like the sun just went out then, something powerful and odd in the way it fell, and the air turned green.

"We gone get a rain, good an' proper," Lodi said.

You could see it coming, too—black columns of it moving in the valley.

Beyond the two grunts at the truck, up a ways where the water was shallow and wide, a squad of troops came out of the bush and forded the river. They took out soap and washed themselves as they crossed. They looked to have been in the bush for some time. They had beards, and hair to their shoulders. They washed themselves and their uniforms, while they still wore them, but they did not ever exactly stop walking.

I asked, "Whatever happened to that big ole boy used to fish here all the time?"

"He's back to the world," Cricket said. "That kid's his replacement." He nodded toward the truck. "The Mexican there with Butch." After awhile he said, "I think he'll be alright. I don't know for sure. He's only 'bout four days old."

"What's his name?" I said.

"He ain't got one yet."

"Firs' night he come heh," Lodi said, "Billy puts 'im on guard duty up dis post see where a mongoose live. Ole mongoose been heh longer'n any a us, an' he know all 'bout what a C-ration is—'cause we feed 'im all da time. You trow out a can, like say you finish witch yer peaches, you trow dat can away, ole mongoose'll run out dere an' grab it wid boat han's . . . look inside see what it is, den mash his face down in't, get him some peach juice.

"So dis kid's on guard duty an' we'd told 'im, 'Hey—watch out fo da rats, man . . . dey big.' An' I guess mongoose did his trick, 'cause nex' mornin', boy's goin', 'Shit . . . is biggest fuckin' rat in di world live up dere. . . ."

Well we were laughing and everything, but the sky kept getting darker and wind came shaking the trees.

Lodi was staring toward the truck.

"Hey, Butch!" he called to the kid with the tattoo, but he didn't hear. He and the Mexican were leaning on a fender and staring at the current as if it were something profound.

The tow-head spoke to me: "See that clearing on the other side, jus' behind the truck there? Look right over Butch's head. . . ."

He pointed to a flat area. I could see the corner of a building, just the corner, nothing else left, and half a wall in another part. The jungle was overtaking it, and what could still be seen was just peeking out of the vines.

"Used to, there was a little village there," the tow-head said. "One the old-timers tole me the gooks there had a butterfly farm. The whole village raised butterflies."

This gave him great pause. After awhile he looked at me evenly and said, "The hell would anybody raise butterflies for you 'spose?"

But the rain started falling good then, came stinging down. I watched as Butch and the Mexican kid got into the truck and rolled up the windows. Pretty soon, from the direction of the Rock Pile, came the muffled sound of rocket and artillery fire.

Charlie would do that, if it got to raining good during the day. There were caves in the mountains across the Z. They had their guns on pulleys, and they would haul them out and fire, and then put them away before anyone could fix on them. At Camp Carroll a month earlier, the Marines stormed a mountain top across the way and captured one of these. It was a PAC 75, a miniature artillery piece manufactured by General Electric. The date stamped on it was 1943. It was in perfect working order.

Now the artillery noise started getting mixed with thunder, and the rain moved toward us in a black curtain from the valley.

"Butch needs t'get out that truck," Lodi said.

It was the last thing I heard clearly against the violence of the storm. For lightning struck and the rain came down then as it must have in Noah's dreams. And in no time, the truck, with those two boys inside, though it hadn't moved, seemed to be moving toward the middle of the river.

We yelled to them, but really you couldn't hear your own voice as it left your mouth. The sound was just torn away. Then it felt like I was falling into the earth, the ground giving way to the rain and the water boiling down the mountainside. The four of us scrambled upward to a place of solid rock. We grabbed on to each other, to stone, root—anything that would hold against the mad downward rush to the river below.

When I looked back to the truck, little of it was visible. I saw this in illuminated moments caused by lightning flash, because otherwise, it was dark, like night had suddenly fallen. The Mexican kid was gone already. Nobody saw how it happened. They never even found his body. Butch was struggling with a door that wouldn't open. He climbed out the window, finally, onto the cab of the truck, the river angry and foaming at his legs. Then it looked that he was standing on the water itself, trying to keep balance there, because the truck was under; you couldn't see it at all. And soon the river swept him away.

The four of us on the bank were huddled together, holding fast to one another, but Lodi called out Butch's name, broke away and started toward the water. Everything was too quick to make a thought for. But there was Lodi, sliding downward to the river, his guiding idea so brave and senseless you could not fix any meaning on what he was doing. And he ran to the water and dove.

He didn't come up, never broke surface again at all. A moment later, the river turned the truck against its grain and rolled it away, end over end. Huge trees came somersaulting by. Fifteen minutes had elapsed, maybe less.

And after awhile the rain stopped, and the sun came out, and on the other side, the monkeys returned to the water's edge. And nothing hadn't changed, except that three more boys were gone, and the river was fatter.

Joe Grind

Anywhere you went in Placencia you'd see Shoestring walking. You'd see him on the road, he'd go by the house several times a day walking the beach, you'd pass him on the sidewalk down in the village. Sometimes he'd be on the old airstrip, walking one end of it to the other, back and forth. He was a dark Creole fella, in his mid-twenties, always in the process of growing dreadlocks. But they never got anywhere on him, and he'd tie shoestrings in his hair, perhaps to mimic the effect he wanted eventually. Shoestrings were only the most consistent item on his head, though. Whatever he happened upon in his walks, if he deemed it appropriate, he'd tie it to his head and continue on his way. He seemed especially partial to baby doll parts he found washed up on the beach. But he'd be ambling about, wouldn't ever look nobody in the eye, wouldn't speak. If you didn't know he was crazy, you might just think him shy, and, for the most part, he appeared totally removed from his environment, whatever it happened to be at the moment, even as he was passing through it. He sometimes interrupted these serene walks, however, with a spectacular jump in the air, at the apex of which he would execute a karate kick at an invisible foe. He might execute this two or three times in a row. These outbursts, I noticed, were occasioned whenever one or more of the village chickens happened to look at him directly.

He seemed harmless enough. Someone told me he lived with his mother. Somebody else said he hadn't always been that way, that he'd been stung by a large scorpion, or maybe it was a near miss, but the scorpion in question was quite large at any rate. Then one day my friend Cattouse told me, "Stay 'way from 'im. He di one da chopped Shakey."

Shakey was a fella you'd see around the village delivering various items in a wheelbarrow. He ran errands. Soon as he got paid, he'd buy a beer. He was drunk most always. The first time I ever saw him was outside Kitty's Place. He was very drunk that day and appeared to be having an earnest, though one-sided, conversation with a crabou tree.

He came up the steps to the bar later on. I was sitting at the first table on the balcony, facing the sea. He needed a light for his cigarette, and I gave him my cigarette to get his lighted with. When he gave mine back, I held it together awhile until he left. He'd mauled it. But he was a very happy person, and he never forgot that I'd helped him light his cigarette. He never forgot anything, I learned, no matter how impaired he was at the time.

But when he came up the steps there to Kitty's, he had this big, lop-sided grin; it wasn't till he was close that you noticed it was augmented by a chop mark to the face, long scarred-over at this point, but quite evident, and another terrible gash on his head, several minor cuts here and there on his arms. The blows to the head, though, you had to wonder how he survived that. It hurt to look at them.

Here's the story of how Shakey happened to get chopped:

It seems there was a kind-hearted Peace Corps volunteer who had once tried to befriend Shoestring, or at least carry on a conversation with him. Her name was Arletta Winterbottom. Shoestring was never known to stand still, so it was a sort of running conversation at best, but as they passed in front of Jene's in downtown Placencia, the youth was heard to ask, "Why do you walk all the time?" Shoestring actually answered her, giving one of his rare public speeches. "Ah grine de carn," he whispered.

Arletta was from a small town in Indiana, a beautiful young lady, pretty face anyway, her hair in a long ponytail—it went all the way down her back—but she was otherwise trapped in a tragically obese body. She was the last of that year's crop of female Peace Corps to dye her hair blonde the village noted, a sign of something that never came clear. She was stationed in the field—out of Blue Creek. She was stout when she came to Belize, but in Blue Creek she'd started smoking ganja with the Mayans, found a love of rice, red beans and tortillas that her hosts thought charming until she started cutting into the supplies they'd laid away for the rainy season. The tortillas especially was a food item she could hardly get enough of, carrying a supply in her backpack even as she spoke to Shoestring. So his reference to corn had struck her as being somewhat mythic in nature.

She stopped then, out of breath, and let Shoestring continue on his way. She went into Jene's and finished off several orders of Johnnie cakes trying to sort it all out. She had on new, roomier clothes she'd purchased recently in Belize City. It was her second set of new duds since she'd come in-country. She was dressed like a white hunter.

Unbeknownst to anyone but himself, however, this encounter with the fat girl had set Shoestring on his ear. Nobody knew this for a good long time. But some noticed, perhaps in retrospect, that whenever the young Peace Corpsman was in the village, Shoestring would load up his hair. It got to be almost a head dress of sorts. This occurred when he was in one of his baby doll periods—all kinds of body parts sticking out his head, and pieces of bright plastic, broken glass, too. It was hilarious and yet slightly alarming. Something was up with him, that was clear. No one dreamed that he'd fallen in love. He never spoke to Arletta again, not in words anyway. But when she was in town, his walking became frantic and confined to a proximity near her whereabouts. If she was eating breakfast at Sonny's say, there'd be Shoestring going by the place about fifteen times, like someone who lived in the windows. He never even looked in, but still, maybe it was his way of being close.

It went on like this for months, which is to say, nothing really happened. Every once in awhile a Brit tourist might be heard to comment, drinking rums for breakfast beside Arletta perhaps, "Who's the fellow with all that rubbish in his hair?" But the village soon lost track of it, and maybe nothing would have come of it at all, except that Arletta got hot on one of the town characters named Russell the Rhymer.

One night at the Cozy Corner, the disco in Placencia, Russell got so high he mistakenly asked Arletta to dance. Arletta was sitting there with her best friend in the Peace Corps, Wanda, another blonde mid-westerner who was stationed in San Pedro on Ambergis Caye, of all places. *Oh, rough duty, I'm sure!* Arletta often commented to herself as she tried to sleep out in the open in her hammock at Blue Creek. *Why not just put her in Miami Beach for Christ's sake.* Well, there was a little jealousy involved. Also, Wanda weighed about one ten. Russell meant to ask her to dance, but it was unclear exactly whom he was speaking to, and Arletta jumped up. By the end of the song she was pretty much madly in love with Russell the Rhymer. He had a funny way of dancing, like a jackknife opening and closing. Nevertheless . . .

Russell had composed several poems for a project in Standard 3, what we'd call 5th grade, and forever after had been dubbed the Rhymer. Nobody called him this to his face unless they were really drunk, because the young, self-conscious poet had grown up into a big, surly Creole man. He weighed maybe 250 at this time, with a big gut. He'd sit on a bar stool with his arms around himself as it were and drink the days away. He felt pretty special about himself. He'd been to L.A. you see.

It wasn't clear what he did in L.A., but he came back with some cash. Show business he hinted, but no one bought that. Later he talked of the carnival like being a carnie was a romantic occupation. The boys at Kitty's watching the boxing matches on ESPN tried to figure it. Maybe he was a weight guesser. Shooting gallery barker. Merry-go-round operator. Then somebody came up with, "He run da focking hot dog stan'." This was probably more like it.

But that entire next week Arletta neglected her duties in the bush and was seen around Placencia with Russell, feeling his muscles and so forth. She wrote her weekly letter home to the folks. If she missed that, they would be upset. She told them she had taken up music. A Creole horn. She complained that it was hard blowing down such a big instrument, but that she was getting the hang of it.

Arletta did not consider herself experienced with men, though, come to think of it, she'd taken on a couple Gerkha soldiers in San Pedro the last time she'd visited Wanda there. She'd taken them both at once. They were small guys she reasoned. The next day she didn't feel too good about herself, but then again, she didn't feel all that bad either. She didn't know much about black people either, though Russell wasn't very dark. The town she'd come from in Indiana, there weren't but two black families out of a population of 11,000. She herself had never spoken to one on any personal level until she came to Belize.

Her only experience with drugs before Belize was all but nil, too. She'd taken L.S.D. once at a bar in South Bend after a Notre Dame football game. She didn't even know what it was, but she took it well—it amused her. The fella who gave it to her came on pretty strong after awhile. She didn't know him very well—she'd just met him several hours earlier—and didn't feel it'd be correct to go to bed with him. Also, if she looked at him any length of time, he'd turn into a lizard. He kept buying her beers, and they had absolutely no effect on her, even if, from time to time, she had to actually clamp her hands over her mouth to stop the laughter. Finally, when her companion turned into a lizard the next time, she said to herself, *Aw hell, I'll just go ahead and fuck a lizard.*

But somewhere in that week of carrying on with Russell, the two of them were spotted by Shoestring. And he stopped walking. He parked himself on the beach just north of the Rasta temple, which was a collection of poles and driftwood and old sails, and sharpened his machet for three days. The Dreads who usually sat there like statues began to shy away from the place.

Now that Friday night, Shakey was reclining on a beach chair out front by the door of the Cozy Corner. He had been acting as the ticket taker, but everyone who had a ticket was now inside. He had his domino game with him, and he was considering about just where he should hide it so he could go in and dance. He was sitting there with one leg crossed over the other, leaning on himself, his beer hand extending over his knee, half a bottle of Belikin there, when all of a sudden Shoestring popped around the side of the building. He knocked the back of Shakey's hand with the flat of his blade, and the beer broke on the sidewalk. It all happened fast, Shoestring walking by him onto the dancefloor. "What da fock!" Shakey said. And his hand hurt like hell, but more pressing than it, he regretted the loss of his drink, and also the deposit on the bottle.

Well in the time it took Shakey to evaluate the situation and to act upon it, Shoestring had walked up behind Arletta, made one slice downward with his machet and neatly clipped off her ponytail. It was about three foot long, and he stood there comtemplating it. Arletta reached behind and touched her scalp and came back with blood on her hand. He'd cut it a little close, see. She turned around and saw Shoestring holding her ponytail and eyeing it in that peculiar batty way of his. Arletta screamed like the Howler monkeys up along the river at dusk. And there was Shakey saying to Shoestring, "Ya cahn't do dat shit, mahn."

That's when Shakey got chopped.

The jail is only a couple doors down from the disco, and pretty soon Jaco, Placencia's only cop, and one of his unpaid assistants and drinking buddies, Elvis, were on the scene. They'd already been there earlier and got drunk, danced a few, were feeling pretty fine about the night; now they had a massacre on their hands. It looked like that anyway, as Shakey was bleeding all over the place. They called in the Brits, who flew Shakey in a helicopter to Belize City and the hospital there. Then Jaco and Elvis combed the village until they came upon Shoestring walking the road along the lagoon. There's an old pigpen there where he sometimes took accommodations for the night. They stopped and looked directly at Shoestring, and he did his karate kick. They were about twelve feet apart at the time, but he did it anyway. Jaco pulled his gun and tried to shoot Shoestring, but the weapon jammed. He and Elvis were trying to figure out what the hell was wrong with it, when Shoestring disappeared on them.

What happened next is the Placencia Police Department called up the Seine Bight cop and asked would he please bring his gun over. Then Jaco went back to the Cozy Corner until the fella from Seine Bight came. He was riding a bicycle, and it took him awhile. Elvis, seeing all the blood again, went home. He decided law enforcement wasn't in his future. He thought it was just that you got drunk for free on the weekends; he hadn't counted on blood. Jaco downed five large glasses of straight rum to calm his nerves. He laid the jammed gun down on the floor underneath his chair. It was a large pistol that seemed to belong to another era.

In the meantime, Shoestring went to his mother's house and tried to chop her, but she got out of there. She went and found the cops her ownself. Shortly after that, the Seine Bight cop wounded Shoestring in the leg, effectively ending his escape, although, at the time, he was eating a mango on his mother's porch and seemed to have forgotten the whole affair.

It came out in the trial what it was all about—that Shoestring had fallen in love, and so on. Because until then, nobody could figure it. Arletta recreated their conversation in court. "He said, 'Ah grine di carn.' " *Joe Grind* is the local name for your wife or girlfriend's backdoor man, and the magistrate, looking at Shoestring, had to smile in spite of himself and his position.

Soon afterwards, Arletta was sent home by the Peace Corps. Russell went back to L.A. for awhile. Shoestring was found guilty of grievous harm and did time—I think it was four years—but he's out now as I've said, he's back in Placencia. And every once and awhile, he and Shakey will have to pass each other in the daily business of life in a small fishing village in Belize.

Top

This was toward the end of our stay at Camp Carroll. Soon enough, we'd start moving, to the Rock Pile, Cam Lo, and we'd end up at an anonymous place called C-2. But right then I'd been in-country nine months and on that mountain the whole time. Here's what happened: The previous night one of our men, this little guy everybody called Glass, had shot himself in the foot. He's probably still hobbling around to this very day, but at the time, he was off the hill and most likely in Japan already, and I recall thinking what a lucky son of bitch he was.

I was no longer on the gun crew then. I had been made the postal clerk for our battery. It was the best job in the battery if you were an enlisted man. I had a jeep to move around in and, to some extent, kept my own schedule. Glass had shot himself out on the perimeter on guard duty. He'd been alone out there. His real name I've blocked out over the years. But he was called Glass because he'd gotten his heart broken so badly by a Dear John letter from home. I'd been the one who handed him the news. The postal clerk didn't have to pull guard duty. I was sleeping at the time and didn't even hear the shot. But I knew what it was like. You had too much time to think out there.

We had a Top Sergeant then everyone called The Gator, mainly because of his disposition. He was part Cherokee, 6 foot 3, all muscle and bone, lanky, leathery, mean as hell and strictly business. Though at night, every night, he drank all the time, and there was this other part about him—he was a good man. This was not something he let on much, though. He just wanted to be known as a hardass, and he was pretty successful at that.

It was all by the book with him. He knew everyone's job. You didn't know how to do something, he'd walk you through. Or say a gunner went down, he'd get up there in the hotseat and take coordinates all night. Or if one of the guns threw a tread or broke down in some other way, he could fix it better than our mechanics. But what endeared him to me was that he took absolutely no shit from the officers. He ran them, just like he ran everyone else. And the whole battery was scared of him.

For some reason, he took a liking to me. He felt at home with me, though why I don't know. We weren't anything alike, not then anyway. But he got me this soft job as postal clerk, I guess just so he could have someone to bullshit with. Before this I'd been humping ammo. The shells weighed 143 pounds. Sometimes the guns fired all night. Then there'd be chores to do during the day. You were pretty much angry all the time and close to madness. So I'd accepted the job quick, believing justly that I had paid my dues.

The job was cake. I could type and knew a little grammar—not much, but more than Top. I'd help him with his paperwork, try to get it straight anyways. He'd grown up in Oklahoma on a dirt farm and never had much schooling. I'd keep an eye out for him at night, see that he got back alright when he went to the club, which was just a bunker where the non-coms got drunk whenever the action was slow. He didn't return to his hootch by a certain time, I'd go look for him. Maybe he'd fallen, and I'd help get him home. I'd be his crutch.

But it wasn't like he'd cut loose with me either. He'd been in the Army since WW II, minus three years he spent as a civilian after Korea, when he sold shoes for a living. He had a long, sharp face, with a dour expression seemingly carved upon it, and you couldn't imagine him selling shoes. He had some great stories about Army life; he didn't have a one about the shoe business. I'd laugh at his stories. It went with the job, I suppose, but they were funny as hell, some of them, though he'd tell them in deadpan. Maybe he'd grin sometimes, a little smile; that was it. He was sort of a deadpan humorist, yet his eyes, it struck me, were often amused. But he didn't, long as I knew him, ever laugh out loud but once, and that's kind of what this story is about.

Now in our battery, we had a monkey. His name was Chico. He looked to be the same kind of monkey that organ grinders have. The story went that a Marine, years ago, had found him chained to the wrist of a dead man. The Marine kept Chico and took care of him until he, the Marine, rotated out. He'd passed Chico on to someone in our battery. See, we were Army, but we were attached to the Marines. Now when that person left, he passed Chico on again, etc. No one knew how long this had been going on except the monkey himself. But this buddy of mine, one of the cooks named Shortround, had Chico for a good long time, and when Shortround went back to the world, he gave Chico to me.

Far as monkeys went, I guess, Chico was just crazier than hell. He'd seen it all, and he was one shell-shocked little guy. The only way to keep him at all calm was to give him beer to drink. He would hold the can with both hands, tip it up and drink hell out of it. He was an alcoholic monkey, you see. He would get hangovers, the shakes, you name it. And he was the second meanest son of bitch around, right behind Top. If Chico decided he didn't like you, say you gave him a beer with just a sip or two left in the bottom, soon as he felt how light that can was, he'd knock it down, then reach out, grab the hand that fed him and bite the hell out of it. He had these long, canine teeth, and buddy he could put it to you.

And really, you couldn't just let him go. He was getting on in years, and like I said, he was crazy.

Now part of the job of being postal clerk was that you sold the beer also. The troops could buy two beers apiece each night. It was warm, but you got used to that. And every night there'd be a line. But the point is, even before I got Chico, he already knew me. I was the guy with all the beer, right?

Well, this particular day I'm speaking of took place near the end of the monsoon season. The Marines had had a big fight down the road two nights back, and they'd kicked ass. Later they sent a deuce-and-a-half truck down there and took weapons off the dead. I was sitting on the ground at the camp over to the right of the piss tubes where you had a nice view of the valley, and I was playing around with Chico. He's sitting opposite me, and I was talking to him and poking him every once in awhile to sort of get him in gear, get his mind off his hangover; he's working through a bad one.

And here comes this deuce-and-a-half full of guns—mostly Kalishnakovs, AK 47's. A couple of Marine grunts started throwing them off the truck, just making a big pile of them on the ground there, maybe twenty meters away.

I watched this awhile, then I turned back to say something to Chico; he's looking at me—maybe there's three feet between us—with that totally startled expression he always had on his face, when all of a sudden, one of the guns thrown down went off.

The bullet went between me and Chico, about eye level. It cut where we sat facing one another right in half.

We both turned our heads just slightly to the left in the direction the bullet went. Then we turned back at the same time, and we looked at each other. And the both of us, I swear, shook our heads in disbelief. It was like we had the very same thought: *Can you fucking believe that?*

I looked at one of the Marines, the one staring at me, but he shrugged, said, "Sorry." It was just one of those things that happened there sometimes. And luckily no one was hurt.

When I told Top about this later was the time when he laughed out loud. He all but had a fit.

He still had ole Glass' boot sitting there on his desk. It had a tiny hole on the top where the bullet had entered and one about the size of a fist in the sole where it came out. He absent-mindedly picked it up and threw it out the window of the hootch and, I suspect, never thought too much more about Glass the rest of his life.

"That jus' beats all," he said. "Shit, I believe you gone straight to heaven when you die. You an' that damn monkey both." And he laughed and laughed.

And I'll tell you, when a man laughs such as that, someone like Top who didn't have a whole lot of practice, it's catching. You get to doing it, too, and you can't stop. You don't even know what you're laughing at. It took me a long while to understand—that it was the first time, in all those months, he'd laughed while Death was looking.

Changing Horses

During the night, Lester Bully had two problems. He'd solved one by burying the colt's mother behind the stables, right where she'd dropped. He'd just dug the hole around her. If you've ever had to dispose of a dead horse, you can better appreciate the enormity of this problem. It had taken most of the night. Bully was a big, nut-brown Creole man, getting on in age, and his muscles and back were tired. He stood there for a moment now opening and closing his large hands.

It was almost daylight in National Stadium, as the horse track was named. Soon the roosters would start crowing around the neighborhood, the joggers would begin to arrive, and the walkers and bicyclists, who shared the track with the horses in these sorry times; horse racing had all but shut down in Belize City.

Bully kept an eye out for his nephew, Chidi, and his cab. He was going to take the colt to Chidi's mother in Cayo. How to get it there was his second problem, though the solution had come to him in the dark. He was going to just load the damn thing in the backseat. He'd have to talk his nephew into it. Cajolery didn't work on Chidi, but cash often hit the spot.

The dead mare was a cherry bay. He'd called her Sheila, since she'd come from Australia originally, though she hadn't ever especially answered to that or to anything else he said. Bully had three sisters and a couple dozen nieces and nephews, and the concept of names had gotten away from him. He'd inherited four horses from his older brother, Granville, who'd passed away several years back. His brother felt fine one day; then a day later he was yellow as corn; then he died. Nobody ever figured out why.

Bully sold two of the horses for living-on money. They were Class A horses, some of the finest in the country at the time. Another one stepped in a crab hole, broke his leg, and had to be put down. Then there was Sheila. She was an old granny horse but still had an eye for the studs. Bully had no idea who sired the colt, but he'd come out pretty—light red with a blond tail and mane. It was half grown now and wouldn't be a big horse at any rate. But the colt was so docile, Bully feared there was something wrong.

Often the horses at the track—there were always at least 6-7 around at any given time—would play in the mornings, race among themselves, scatter the joggers. But this colt just stood around mostly like it had been hypnotized. It was either a truly gentle being or a simpleton. Bully hadn't yet figured out which. All he knew for sure was that he'd gotten damn sick of the horse business. And presently he owed three months back rent for the stable. The stables at the National Stadium resembled a collection of chicken coops. He had no intention of paying this particular bill.

Chidi's mother was also Bully's sister, though she didn't always admit to that. She'd been put out about not getting a share of the horses in the first place. So he'd give her this one, make amends. The woman got on well with animals. Much better than with humans, certainly. She had a chicken that followed her around constantly and a yellowhead parrot she was taken with which laughed maniacally all day and drove everyone else nuts. Her life was guided by superstition and dread. She was positive their brother had died of snake bite, even though the doctor had ruled that out. Since then, to get even with snakes in general, she wore dice made of bone in her hair. How did that add up? And even if it did somehow, it just looked so damn stupid. She wouldn't go swimming on Good Friday as she feared being turned into a mermaid. "On an' on wi' dat shit," Bully spoke aloud just then.

He ran his hand through his gray hair, put his straw hat back on. He knew everybody had at least one black page in their book, but she owned nearly the whole dark story. There was no arguing upon such folly. None of her doings made sense to Bully, but mortality had begun to weigh on him of late. He was getting old. They all were. Well, and it was time to make up, to set things right in the family.

Bully looked around. He often stayed out here late into the evenings, playing cards with Sugar Reneau, the night watchman. It was quiet then. Sugar only had one arm; he played slow. Bully'd listen to the sea, watch the night herons hunting in the marsh grass. A couple old rummies Sugar knew, they'd wander in late and sleep on the benches of the grandstand. The wood was worn smooth by the past. The grandstand had a tin roof. It held maybe two hundred and fifty people on race days, but anytime recently it wasn't hard to find a seat. Racing had moved up to Burrell Boom. Of the horses that stabled year-round now, only one of them was a thoroughbred. The rest were just pets. They'd run in the Village Race mabye, where they saddled up the work horses.

The last race here—on Baron Bliss Day—there was not even one pretty woman in the crowd. Not one rich man. And the place itself was just falling down, no straight lines left in its construction, and many of the boards that made the fence around the track were rotted or already gone. He saw Sugar sleeping in a lawn chair, his one arm cradling the 16-gauge he always had with him. Behind his back, people called him Lefty. Even he had fallen apart, see?

Now athletes and health nuts were out here day in and day out. It wasn't right for a race track. Bully'd sit around watching them in disgust. He'd drink Belikin Stout, smoke cigars, spit. A month ago, he'd watched as three fat Creole women walked the track, their hair in curlers; one of them held a lemon-colored umbrella. All the women wearing curlers around town—was that what passed for style now? he wondered. And the fellas with their ballcaps on sideways? Lord! That day sort of marked the end of the line for Lester Bully. The track had gone sad on him.

He was chopping some long grass to take with when he saw Chidi's headlights. Chidi was jug-eared and homely, but he had turned out pretty good, considering. He'd got some strangeness from his mother—they were cut from the same cloth, though the patterns were somewhat different. He was just odd mostly in an amusing way. Always some preposterous article of clothing. And here it was—a black billycock hat with a piece of white telephone cord wrapped around it several times, the receiver still attached and perched on his shoulder. He was drinking cashew wine out of a blue bottle. Bully opened the back door of the LTD and threw in the grass.

"Tio Bully—what di fock?" He started to carry on in Creole.

"Talk English," Bully said. The Creole had gotten so weird around town he couldn't get to most of it. He just wasn't savvy no more.

He explained how they were going to load the colt into the backseat. "Take it to your Mama's. Hurry up now 'fore it get light." He handed a blue note to Chidi. Chidi took the hundred dollar bill to the lantern, looked it over for a full minute. He looked at the front and the back. It was like when a baby first discovers its hands.

The colt thrashed around for awhile, then found the grass and got comfortable. Bully jumped into the shotgun seat.

"Let's go, Chidi. We got a long ride." Neither Bully nor the colt had gotten much rest that night, and by the time Chidi's cab rattled through the graveyard on the Western Highway, they were both asleep.

Some three hours later down that same highway, outside a village named Black Man Eddie, two children sat under a tree at the side of the road. Beside them was a dead dog in a wagon.

The young girl was named Blanca, and the boy was Ben Louviere. Ben had been in Belize exactly a month. He was twelve years old, going on thirteen. He was from Canada, and his parents had bought an orange grove in this little village. Blanca was their neighbors' daughter. She was fourteen, but to Ben looked much older, a woman almost. And she seemed to know the score about things.

Blanca's family lived in an extremely small house to the front of the Louviere's 20 acres. The house was beside the entrance to the grove. She was going to church shortly, and she had on her Sunday dress, a frilly yellow outfit, pink socks and white sandals. She was Spanish, with dark curly hair, and Ben was smitten by her beauty.

They'd just recently become friends. Blanca had invited him to eat dinner with her family the day before. Far as Ben could tell, there were four adults and two smaller children than Blanca living in that tiny house. There were visitors coming and going, but he thought that was about the size of it. Blanca's father was barely alert. He had what she called a *goma*—a fierce hangover.

Ben knew about such things, being from Canada.

They'd eaten chicken that meal, and something named cow's foot soup, a dish traditionally eaten on Saturday, she'd explained. There was still hair on the hoof, Ben noticed, which had worked to the detriment of his appetite. Afterwards, what scraps left were thrown into a bowl outside for the cats. But the cats were off somewhere, and the biggest toad Ben'd ever seen approached the bowl and partook. The toad must have weighed two pounds. She called it by name. The image of it with a chicken bone hanging out of its mouth stayed with him. It was disconcerting somehow.

Now he and Blanca had come together again over this dead dog. The dog lay in a little red wagon beside them. They'd hauled it off the road, where it'd been struck in the night. The dog was black-and-white spotted, skinny and stiff.

A big-bellied, white-haired man with tan skin and a cane had come up to them and regarded the dog briefly. He'd poked it with his cane.

"I never liked him," was all that he said. Then he went back to his house.

The two had decided to take responsibility for the dog, but now they weren't exactly sure how to handle it. They sat by the side of the road under an avocado tree discussing the problem.

"We'll need a shovel," Blanca offered.

They looked around for a place to dig. It all looked rocky.

"We'll have a burial service," she said.

"It's just a dog," Ben said. Not much of one either, to his way of thinking.

"Everything has a soul," she said. She said *everyting*. No one seemed able to pronounce "th" here. This appeared to be a national affliction.

Ben had never thought too much on souls before. He'd entered a school run by Mennonites and had to take Bible studies. This past Friday, the teacher discussed the Trinity. The Holy Ghost had stumped him. The Dove and the Tongues of Fire. He still didn't get it. He wasn't sure he wanted to.

A dark Creole kid walked by them then. A rangy kid, eighteen or so. He said to Blanca in passing: "I'll be by some night. Keep it neat."

"I cyan," she said.

"It bad fu so lie when you so young," he answered back. Then he smiled big.

Ben thought, What in the world was that all about?

Blanca blushed. Then she studied the dog some more.

She was very clear-skinned, though not nearly as white as Ben, he noted. He figured he was just about the whitest boy in the country right now. His skin appeared to be made of plaster. The black kids at school had given him the nickname Cheese. Most all the Mennonite cheese was white cheddar.

He asked her now, "You know about the Holy Ghost?"

Blanca didn't want to appear to not know. She thought it better, in most instances, to say something, anything, rather than to admit ignorance. She went to church with her mother every Sunday, but, then again, it was a social occasion; she didn't pay so much attention to what the preacher said. He was only a preacher on Sunday. The other days of the week, he sold used cars and dabbled in the currency exhange.

"You mean the Holy Goose, don't you?" she countered.

"Goose?"

"Yes," she said. "We have one. Di white one." She saw he was having trouble with that and changed the subject. "We can jus' trow dis dog back in a field. An' John Crow will come clean 'im up."

"What about his soul, then?"

She regarded the dog.

"He has a very skinny soul, if at all," she said. "But . . . I don't care. We'll have to build a cross. Do you have a hammer?"

Just then, Lester Bully, Chidi and the colt went by in the taxi.

Chidi had the telephone cord wrapped around his head and the receiver on his shoulder, expecting a call of some sort. He was taking a pull on that blue bottle. He was regarding himself in the rearview mirror. The road was secondary at the moment, like the car was on its own. Bully was still asleep and, slouched down in the seat, nothing was visible but for his straw hat, which seemed to float there by itself. The colt had its face out the back window on the shotgun side of the car, a long piece of grass hanging out of its mouth like a real hayseed.

As the car sped by, the colt, with its enraptured expression, looked back upon Ben Louviere. It wrinkled up its nose, as if perhaps saying something to him.

Blanca missed the whole thing.

Ben said, "What the hell was that?"

Blanca looked at the car disappearing down the road. She saw the green license plate.

"It was a taxi," she said.

Jesus Murphy, Ben thought. He put his hands to his T-shirt and plucked it off his body a couple times. He was hot. It was February. Little more than a month ago, he'd been shoveling snow. It'd been 30 below zero then. There were whiteouts in their little town of Flin Flan, Manitoba, so that you could no longer see the neighbors' houses. These would last for days, until you began to doubt anyone else was actually out there. They'd had wolves in their backyard. But none of that seemed nearly so strange as this new country.

In the Gare At Bayonne

"Did anybody in your family ever make it all the way through without dying?"

—Russell Moore, age 7, a question for his father

The train pulled into the gare at Bayonne and stopped. We would have a twenty minute layover before we headed to Spain. There wasn't but one old French lady, Jane and myself left in the coach. It was 6:00 in the evening, September sunlight. We'd left Arles at 9:44 that morning, followed the Pyrenees across southern France. From Friday through Sunday we'd been to the Feria du Riz in Arles—their rice festival. We'd stayed at the Hotel du Forum, room 47, a room that seemed as if Van Gogh might have just been evicted, but we hadn't spent much time in it. The party was outside and didn't stop for the night. Now in Bayonne we stayed in the coach. We stood up, stretched our legs and sat back down. We just sat there.

Looking to my left, I see this out the train window: A large sign on the wall that says BAYONNE, and under it, a big man in a dark red sweater sitting on a bench. He had a cart he'd built—some dresser drawers, a dolly under them, and it's all held together by rope. The man is not thin, as you'd expect someone to be living on the street. His face is beefy and red. He has a green bottle of wine, a two liter bottle, larger than most, at his side. He uncorks it, takes a drink.

Another very old and infirm fella comes walking into the picture from the south. He's wearing a shabby gray suit and black beret. He walks so very slowly, it's almost like a comedy sketch. He's half-stepping it, if that. I don't think he's been drinking, but maybe just a little. I think mostly that he is truly antique.

From the same direction, Robert Smith enters the scene. He's walking at a normal pace, yet in comparison to the old guy in the beret, he seems to be moving rapidly, and soon passes him. Now there are three on this stage, and no one else will enter. What follows takes place some 25 feet from me.

Robert is younger now and slightly taller. He hasn't shaved for a couple days, his hair is a little long, that same light sandy color, disheveled and amassed on his broad head. He has on a blue windbreaker and ghastly, lime green pants. It's not a wardrobe you would be inclined to on purpose. Maybe he'd found the clothes or somebody had given them away. He looks fairly healthy. This is a bit odd in that he's been dead and buried going on five years now.

Robert approaches the man in the red sweater and asks for a smoke. He makes the gesture—holds his hand in front of his mouth as if he had a cigarette between his first two fingers, moves his hand back and forth. The other fella shakes his head *no.* Robert sits down on the bench sideways so that he's facing him. The two discuss it. It's obvious they don't speak the same language. The fella in the red sweater throws up his hands in frustration finally, takes Robert to the trashbin about ten feet away. He fishes out a crumpled pack, holds it up. Robert looks at it, then looks in the trashbin.

And you have to keep in mind the antique fella in the beret is still crossing the scene. He had moved, now, even with the bench, where the other two have since returned. He's moving, but not exactly. He seems to have slowed a bit, and he is not getting anywhere.

On the bench, the fella in the red sweater has a drink from his big bottle. Robert perks up, takes an interest in this. There's more discussion between them. Hard to tell what they're getting at, but then Robert hurries off. The other fella watches him go. He takes another drink.

The old guy in the beret is still moving past. I finally understand that the W.C. is just beyond the trash can. He's headed there, right? He's got to take a leak. He appears to be muttering to himself. He's moving at one mile per day, and just then stops to adjust his hat.

Time seemed to be in total suspension out there. A stillness like in a painting. Now it started up inside our coach. The old lady in the aisle across from us, who had caught the train at Lourdes and read magazines since, took a packet from her traveling bag, containing goat cheese and bread, and cut the cheese with a small folding knife. The cheese had not traveled well, and the goat came over and took a seat beside me. I guess she noticed me tossing my head, sniffing the air. She laughed quietly and said to Jane in French: "*Ce fromage sent comme une jeune fille negligee*."

I looked at Jane.

"She said, 'This cheese smells like a neglected young lady.' "

I turned toward the window again. Here comes Robert back, and he has two glasses. The fella in the red sweater is suddenly expansive. He opens one of his dresser drawers and takes out bread. He takes out cheese. The cheese is wrapped in butcher paper. He cuts it with a big kitchen knife. He fills Robert's glass with red wine. Robert breaks off pieces of bread from the loaf. He stuffs his mouth with bread. Cheese. He motions for the other fella to fill his own glass with wine, too. The man laughs, takes a long drink from the bottle.

Just then the old guy in the beret tripped on a cobblestone. He literally flies headlong the last ten feet to the W.C., hits a corner of the open doorway with a shoulder, and spins into its depths.

Jane is laughing. She'd seen this but hadn't seen him trip, only thought he couldn't wait on himself any longer.

Robert and his partner on the bench take this in momentarily also. They crane their necks. The fella in the red sweater wheels his thumb toward the W.C., raises his eyebrows, as if to say—What's with him? Then they go back to the business at hand. They eat and drink. Laugh. It's a great railroad feast. I'd never seen Robert eat so when he was alive. Drugs, alcohol—he had a great hunger there, but food never concerned him too much.

There's another discussion after the meal. Robert takes some coins from his pocket, studies them. Turns them over, like maybe their value is different on the other side. The man in the red sweater counts them, too. They don't add up for him. He holds his bottle to the light, shows Robert how much is gone. He considers the bottle with some sadness. Robert looks at his coins again, shakes his head. He's baffled. The other fella stands, traces a large number 7 on the wall behind him.

Our train started. Another train, a long freight, shunted onto an adjacent track, came between us and the scene as it went past. Then we were moving, too.

Jane asked me, "Who did that young guy back there remind you of?"

At the cemetery behind the Baptist church in Turkey Creek, Florida, the morning Robert was buried, a similar long freight had passed close by, its loud whistle blocking the preacher's words who spoke over him. I'd rather listen to a train than a preacher any day. And I had Robert's own words in my mind just then. Sometime after he loaded the .38 on Christmas Eve, he'd recorded in his notebook—*I haven't seen my friends lately. I'll have to call them together again.* And I was remembering that he'd come to our house at the lake not so long ago. He'd broken through to his old self. It was our last good time together. A night during which it was hard to imagine life ever again taking a serious turn. The sadness that had overtaken him, it seemed to me then, couldn't endure. It was just a laugh that needed to be rebuilt.

The preacher didn't know Robert. But there were many who knew him well and loved him there that day. Any of us could have said it better, and we did say it, one to another.

I'd taken the notion, that late December morning, Robert caught that freight, had gotten the hell out of there.

Fish Tales

Back one Sunday in 1923, a man by the name of Fritz Friebel, who lived in San Antonio, Florida, skipped church that morning and caught a 20 pound 2 ounce large mouth bass. He was fishing with two of his buddies. They were taller than him, because he was a squat man, but to give you some idea how big this bass was, it stretched from his waist to the top of his boots.

Far as anyone knows, this is the second largest bass ever caught in the world. No one in Florida ever got close to it since. It's still on the books—one of the few things in the state which hasn't changed during that time.

Fritz was wading that day. Them ole boys fishing with him said he kind of liked to get up to his neck in it. He wasn't a fly fisherman, but neither was he a live-bait man. He caught his bass on a Creek Chub Bait Company Straight Pikie Minnow. I've always admired the name of that plug.

He caught it in one of the many lakes around San Antonio. He never said exactly which one. And after showing it off in downtown Tampa for several days in a block of ice, he returned to San Ann and did what they still do there with fish—he and his family ate it.

I was discussing this one afternoon with Pat Rosh. Now Miss Pat is a bartender at the local Knife and Gun Club in San Ann and, as such, one of the leading historians of tall tales in the area.

"My husband had a theory on it," she said. "That we all been tryin' to catch up with Fritz ever since, an' the only way we can do it is to lie like hell."

A sort of contemplative mood made camp right then and there at the bar as Pat continued:

"The bass ain't gettin' that big no more," she said. "They jus' gettin' weirder."

When she said it, I took out my notebook. I could sense a fish tale about to be wove.

"This was out at Chassahowitzka," Pat began.

"How do you spell that?"

"I believe it's with two s's," she said. "Well, we was out on the river, an' it was about dusk, jus' dark enough for us to run lights."

"You had lights on the boat?" I asked.

"We had lights on our heads, the kind that's run by batt'ries, regular headlamps like miners wear. Now to tell you the truth, we weren't even fishin'. It was when we had our huntin' camp up there, an' we was jus' goin' on down the river with the tide. It's brackish water there.

"This was the creek part after we got past the mouth of the Gulf. Then we looped on down another creek, an' jus' about there somethin' hit me right up side the head. Staggered me. I'm not gonna say what I said when it hit me. But I felt about knocked out, 'cause it hit me right in the temple. An' I jus' almost fell down.

"Now my husband was there, an' he said, 'My God, look-it here,' an' sure enough it was a bass. We'd had mullet jump in the boat before, but this was the first time a bass ever did. We took it back to the camp an' weighed it out. It was six an' a half, almost seven pounds.

"An' I was black and blue where it hit me, an' wore a mark there for two, three days after."

Now I don't recall exactly which of the boys it was, either Buddy or Burt or Pee Wee, but one of them spoke as follows:

"Pat, I believe what we might have here is a world record of sorts, seein' as how you caught this bass on zero-pound test line."

And another said: "She was tryin' to catch it in her teeth."

And the third said: "What watt bulb was that you had on yer head?"

Pee Wee said that. And I have to interject something here. Pee Wee had come in just ten minutes earlier. He's this little sawed-off Norwegian, by way of Minnesota originally.

He'd walked in there, said, "What y'all up to?"

Buddy looked him up and down, said, "Same as you I guess, about five foot."

Burt commented, "We was doin' pretty good till you come."

Pee Wee turned to Pat and she advised, "This is by invitation only."

In other words, there was, at all times, a healthy skepticism among this crowd.

Well Miss Pat, as always, took but a small serving of their backtalk, then looked at me and said straight out:

"Jimmy, I swear it's true."

Several days passed before I heard the second tale. And I must preface this tale with a warning. The boy telling it is a carnie I've known for some time. He lives at a trailer park on Lake Pasadena. Many years ago he invented an important carnival attraction. You remember that wagon that shouted: LIVE VIETNAM RAT.

Well that's dated now, but in some circles he's still quite famous for it. I can't mention this boy's name because he says I have to pay him then. And he's married to a Lousiana woman named Rough Baby, but that's another story entirely and not one we should go into. Now what I'm getting to is this: His normal conversation is somewhat colorful and lawless.

I tried to explain the situation to him.

"I'm on assignment," I said.

"What's that mean?" he asked.

"Don't cuss," I said.

In answer he threw out a salty colloquialism or two. Just by chance, an ambulance went by then, and we listened to its siren.

"There goes your ride," he said.

"Look here, now," he went on, "if I can't tell this in my own way, I'm going to squander a great deal of its flavor."

We went back and forth on it, but finally he allowed that he would do the best he could.

Now knowing him to be a home-made philosopher and practitioner of the fish tale, I took out my notebook and began to question him about the genre itself.

"I have a quote of yours, let me see if I can find it." And I read this back to him: *The size of the tale is in direct proportion to the oddness of the circumstances surrounding the catch.*

"I said that?"

"Yes, you did. I've got it right here in my notes."

"Was I drinking when I said it?"

I just rolled my eyes on that. I'd never once in my life known him without a drink in his hand.

"You let that run long enough, I guess it'd catch on to what I meant. But ain't no matter." And he mulled over his thoughts awhile. He pushed back his hair. He said, "I tell you what . . . other'n that, the only common ingredients I can see to any fish story are these—it has to be made out of good yarn, an' at the conclusion, the yarn-spinner must swear up and down it's true.

"Now the best tales, you walk away from them an' don't know if you heard the truth, or if you've been had.

"It all hinges on the nature of the creature itself. For many a time the bass are stronger an' wiser than can be explained. Far as tryin' to figure 'em, there ain't no use in it. Or say you was to compare the Florida bass, in terms of meanness, to your average land animal—well, it's this part rattler an' that part mule.

"Sure . . . an' they're fine eatin', too. One of the best. But then after you eat them, the characteristic large mouth of the species is somehow mystically transferred to those who made the catch. Now in human beings we have come to call this *exaggeration*. . . ."

Then he started his tale.

"This occurred during the harvest moon. Now Baby, she'd baked a chicken for dinner that evening, an' you know how she cooks everything all hot in the Cajun way?

"Well about one o'clock that night, the moon was full and real strong, jus' comin' down like starch, an' we couldn't sleep. So I thought I'd go out an' catch some catfish. I got my pole, grabbed a chicken wing, an' we headed to the dock.

"I threw out my line, an' me and Baby was jus' standin' around there talkin' for about a half hour, but I wasn't getting no bites. So I started reelin' in, see if my bait'd got stolen or what.

"Now about halfway in, I felt somethin' hit at it, an' I pulled back hard an' set the hook. Felt somethin' good. Heavy. I thought it was a big ole catfish. An' I'll tell you, it put up a fight.

"But I get it up close there, an' I see it's a bass, a nice one. We got it in the net, an' it was a four an' a half, five pound bass."

"On a chicken wing?" I said.

"A chicken wing. An' we're admirin' it and laughin'. But I went to take the hook out of its mouth—only it wasn't in its mouth. So we got to lookin' around on the thing, an' . . . I swear this is true, I'd snagged that bass right square in the asshole.

"An' I'll say it again—this is a fish tale, but it ain't no lie. You ask Baby if you want."

Rough Baby said:

"Let me explain you. I mean . . . you should see dat feesh *jomp!*"

There you have it. The next installment in this odd-angled look at Florida wildlife will focus on the softshell turtle, another of those delicacies of table and folklore.

The Good Doctor

A psychiatrist shot himself in the head recently in our town. He used a .45, so there was no mistaking his intentions. The event took place in his office at the Mental Health Center. He was, among his other duties there, a suicide prevention counselor.

The holidays had come on; December rained cold, lead-gray. None of his professional colleagues foresaw the tragedy. There was a general inability to understand it. *He did not seem like the type of man to take his own life. A lot of things don't add up.* That was how they put it. In the same way lightning is said to imprint on a man's body the picture of the tree under which he has been struck, they all wore the same dark countenance.

There was initial concern about his clients. Some of these felt guilty for making him shoulder their problems; others spoke of betrayal. Still others said nothing at all, and these were watched closely. Most everyone who knew him, though, allowed that he was a good doctor. He was, so our local paper reported, very knowledgeable at prescribing the correct medication for any particular shade of mental illness. He was considered an expert in this regard. Of his patients interviewed, one said quite simply, and perceptively I thought, even though it amused me no end, "He's through the hard part now."

Soon enough, particulars of the doctor's life began to circulate in our town. No suicide note had been found. He had moved here four years ago from parts unknown. He hadn't turned to therapy until his 40's (he was 56 when he died) and had an early career in theatre. He was a homemade chef of some ability, who liked to barbecue for friends at his house tucked away in the swamp off Bay Road. I drove by there recently out of curiosity. It's a fine, old house with gingerbread lattice work along the porch. Two century-old cedars stood guard over and shaded it. Once white, it had gone black with mold and spotted by lichen, and its color and the color of the tree trunks had become the same. The small open space in front, where patches of light fell and shifted, was covered in leather leaf and maiden hair fern, and as I sat in the driveway with the car motor turned off, three turkey hens entered there and began scratching the earth. It had a quality of legend about it, I thought—a house you'd read about in the Grimm Brothers.

The Clarion ran a full article on the doctor, which took up most of the paper, and a second, shorter piece a week later, along with his obituary. It was a big story in our town, as, truly, nothing much ever happens here. Usually our media events have to do with accidents at the paper mill, or catches of large snook or tarpon.

The paper comes out once a week. When the initial article appeared, the first Thursday after the New Year, one of my favorite idlers, Buddy Cawthon, was the only customer in the bar at the time, it being 10:30 in the morning. He'd just picked up his Social Security check from the post office. Buddy was a carpenter in his working days; he'd built this bar a quarter century ago and had retained a fondness for it ever since. Lean and withered now, with the face of a turtle, a white mustache, he was reading the doctor's story and commenting on some of its oddities.

"The guy liked to bake bread."

"Read further."

His finger traced the print.

"He published mystery stories under the pen name . . . Audrey Harper."

Buddy raised his eyebrows.

"One of his books was called *The Street of Early Sorrows.* Never read it," Buddy added. "Here's his latest—*The Left Bank of Elsewhere.*" He said the title aloud several more times, to see if it might gather sense to him in the retelling. "Wonder what he was getting at there—you read that one?"

"Can't say that I have."

"Me neither," Buddy said.

Very likely he had not read a book since high school, in the early '40's, and then only when coerced. He pushed his reading glasses back up on his nose and studied Frankie's photograph on the third page. "It's her alright." After awhile he said, "Listen to this, Ben—'She described her relationship with the doctor as platonic, a . . . a . . .' How would you say that word?"

"Psychic."

"A psychic bond?"

He looked at me.

I side-stepped a reply, shrugged. I don't volunteer information. To let on you know such things in this town only brings you sadness and funny looks.

"I never heard Frankie talk like that," Buddy said. "Where'd she get them words?"

"From him, I guess."

"You mind I open the door?" he asked. "It's always so smoky in here." He propped the front door open with a chair, sat back down and lit a cigarette. He soon lost interest in the article and moved on to the crossword puzzle. For the next forty-five minutes, he would ask me puzzle questions, then, when he finished, proudly claim that he had solved it.

But the doctor's story had caught my interest, and later on I looked through it again.

As noted, of his professional associates, none had seen this business coming. (The Health Center is a large affair that serves the entire county. I know one of the doctors, Warren Greenhouse, fairly well—I grew up with him, went to high school with him. He wears his ties knotted hard at the neck. I always thought he felt life was something that could be planned. He has a way of talking, so very measured and slow, plus he moves his lips so seldom they appear to have only a decorative function, the notion of ventriloquism arises, one begins to feel things cannot go on like this much longer, the mind moves serenely towards violence . . . . The total effect is of someone with his soul in a straightjacket. The last time we spoke, he seemed only moments away from slipping into catatonic rapture. I'm not sure why I mention this, as, surely, he cannot be representive of the whole.) They knew he had been saddened recently by the death of a woman who, he said, was a dancer, someone he had intended to move in with, but they didn't know her. And, truth be owned, there is not one woman in the entire town you could actually refer to as *a dancer.* Yet, as it turned out, this was the way he ran his life, having little pockets of acquaintances here and there, and none of these knew of the others.

He had a daughter from a previous marriage, which had ended in divorce. Three days after her father's suicide, the daughter arrived in town by train, a 37-year-old film editor from Burbank, California, with a punk haircut, the hair polychromatic and dyed as if by Easter egg coloring. She met with her father's colleagues at the Health Center, sorted through his belongings in the house, had trouble getting his pick-up truck started. Few in our town had ever seen anyone from Hollywood in real life. They stared at her, unfortunately, much like cattle. "It's hard to imagine there are places like this still around," she told a reporter. A last letter she had sent her father was found unopened in the doctor's mailbox. No mention was made of its content.

A furious wind struck our town for two days and nights while she was here. Before it hit, there was dead stillness, a peculiar hollowness to everything. Then it came from the west, over the Gulf, pushing a long silver wall of rain. When the rain stopped, curtains of spindrift veiled the bay. By night it had blown the stars out of the sky. Small craft warnings were posted, and the bar filled with idled shrimpers, oyster pickers, mullet men, a smuggler or two. Winter storms are not particularly uncommon to this part of Florida, but this one was noteworthy. I slept in my clothes those nights, afraid the roof would go on my house. The storm yanked at the doors and windows like something very large out there in delirious abandon.

In his will, along with stating that he wanted to be cremated (I don't know about you, but I have always looked upon this as a small version of hell, a little warm-up, as it were), the doctor spoke of a toy. He described it as a teddy bear with a red shirt-button sewn on for a nose, left to him by his mother, apparently when she abandoned her family while the doctor was still an infant. Nothing was said at all of the doctor's father, as if he had no antecedents in this respect, which, as we know, doesn't often occur. The staff at the paper is quite good in many ways, and yet they have lapses. For instance, it was mentioned twice that the doctor had few male friends. I took the second as a typo. The paper is still type-set by hand and run off on a press that would not feel out of place at the end of the 19th century, and it retains several truly antiquarian looks, one of which is a *Poets Corner.* At any rate, his daughter found this careworn toy in the possession of one Frances Stewart.

Ours is a small community, the winter population 6,000 at most, but none of the doctor's more prominent friends had ever heard of Ms. Stewart and didn't meet her until after his death. She was a former client living in a cottage near the timber-yard at the south end of town, the paper said, a single mother of three, and, as the photograph of her showed, a large blonde with an ample nose. (Ms. Stewart is an old friend, known as Frankie at the bar—more on this aspect in a moment.) He had been with her the weekend before his death. "He had trouble swallowing," she related.

Several of our town authorities commented on the suicide. The preachers weren't too happy about it, of course, and they expressed this, if not eloquently, at some length. The mayor said, "Folks in this community are willing to help one another when help is needed. But you have to ask." He owns an auto repair shop and added, in a metaphor befitting his trade, "The doctor did a lot of good for others, but I don't believe he was getting his own batteries charged." One source, who wished to remain anonymous, said, "I have only profound respect for his choice." An "anonymous source" in this paper are code words for the editor, either throwing in his two cents worth, or, in this case I believe, playing devil's advocate. It had its effect, as several letters to the editor followed, sparking a mild debate around town on the nature of life and death.

Well I'm a bartender, and, as such, an unofficial, and perhaps better informed, historian of the goings-on around here. People tell things to bartenders you won't read in the newspapers, and I have a decidedly different angle on the doctor. I recognized him from photos in *The Clarion.* He visited my place of employment twice, though until I read that he was a doctor, I had no idea what he did for a living. But I knew what he drank and some other items about him, too. The monotony of certain occupations, mine very much included, forces people to become humorists in order to retain their sanity. And though the doctor's was a sad case, I found a great deal of unintentional humor connected to it. Here's what I mean:

I am, as I said, well acquainted with Frances Stewart. She's Frankie to me and everyone else around here. She accompanied the doctor to the bar on his first visit. She drops in on us two-three nights a week, by herself, usually, though men come and go in her life. I'm no longer interested in learning their names; they don't last long enough to get to know. She has children, but they're grown, the youngest being 19, I believe. He's the only one still in town. He occasionally sports a ring in his nose like a bull. He has his mother's nose and looks quite impressive, if you're into that sort of thing, and, as many of our young people, persists in dressing like a rodeo clown. He has, several times, had trouble with grand theft auto. He would only steal when very drunk and was in the habit of leaving badly written apology notes in the vicinity of where the car used to be, not having the time to speak to the owner in person. He did everything but sign these notes and was soon apprehended. The last time he came to the bar he had cash, a jaundiced face, and ground his teeth continuously. I'd hazard to say that he's cultivating a new habit of some sort. He used the cash to get his mother drunk.

Frankie drinks an uncommon amount, every day I imagine, but she doesn't handle alcohol well. She'll go absolutely sodden or, much worse, become loud. In this state she is fond of referring to herself as a "boozehound" and then, often as not, follows with any number of doggish yips. When she offers this, we immediately cut her off. Personally, I don't care to see a woman in this condition. To get drunk, act like an asshole, I think is a man's job. But this is neither here nor there.

She brought the doctor to the bar one night. He was a big, shambling fella, not big-boned, but quite heavy, with a large, pock-marked face, somewhat bloated, and a nose like a strawberry—the features of a committed drunk I should say—and he dressed like a fisherman, or one of the farmer/ranchers from around here, who, although they have money, do not often reflect it in their sartorial tastes. He had no sun on him, however, so I took him for a visitor from the North.

He was balding, combed his graying hair forward on his head, and had a beard that was very neatly trimmed. And he was an affable sort, all but determined to make conversation with those around him. Though, these boys come in here, many learned their social skills in various exercise yards around the county and don't take readily to strangers. I've seen men come in here ten years before they were accepted.

Frankie introduced us. If I caught his name at all, I immediately lost it. Right off he goes, "Hey, Ben, you horny ole bugger. How you doin'? I've heard a lot about you. . . ." And so on. He shook my hand as though trying to prime it. How droll, I thought.

Then he ordered wine. Wine? This is a whiskey and Busch place, and bar-well whiskey at that. But I dug up a bottle—red, 3/4 full, of questionable vintage to start with, and who knows how long it'd been around. He wanted it anyway, so I poured him a glass. He held it up to the light, took a sip. Then he commented on its qualities. "I'll tell you, Ben," he said, "thin . . . and a bit sour." I tried it. "You're right," I agreed. "It's a barbaric little wine. Maybe some Red Hots would help it out, take the edge off." He started with Red Hots, went to hardboiled pickled eggs, found those to his liking and finished the jar, had some pretzels and peanuts, then a double order of fries. "You got some pepper gravy put on them fries?" he asked. He stuck a few Slim Jims in his pocket for later. After his demise, the paper mentioned some of the items he was interred with—his daughter's letter, the toy, etc. I was thinking they should have buried him with a fork.

After he finished eating, he switched to beer and started smoking Frankie's cigarettes. Whereas he took the wine slow, the beer he drank very fast and, after each one, seemed a bit impatient for the next. And I wouldn't have taken him for a doctor. I make it a practice not to inquire, simply because of the nature of our clientele, as to what anybody does for a living. But a doctor would be the last thing I'd take this guy for. Maybe a root-doctor. *Catch a hoppy toad an' blow yer breath into its mouth each mornin' just 'fore the sun inspires the east so that the willies can't take holt of you.* We have a few of them around. Because he didn't talk like an educated man, but rather took pains not to. He seemed to just want to be a regular Joe, without exactly knowing how. Still, he slipped once and used a word that was so unusual—I can't recall it at the moment. Maybe it will come to me. But anyway, he didn't act even close-on to a doctor. They said in the paper, too, that he didn't have any health problems so far as anyone knew, but he looked to be at least 80 pounds overweight and, from time to time, was sweating his ass off that night, even though the place is cold enough to hang meat.

For the next half hour, I noticed he kept glancing over to the guy sitting next to him, giving him a hard look. I asked finally, "What's the problem?" He kind of takes me aside, says, "Keep an eye on this guy will you? I think he's drinking my beer when I ain't looking." The man beside him was Moody Wohlers. Moody is one of our unfortunates comes in the bar, only has one ear. He lost the other in a car accident, having been thrown from the vehicle and rubbed it off on the pavement. It took some of his wits, also, but left him with a nice settlement, which he doles out parsimoniously. He can nurse a beer half the night. He doesn't even drink his own beer, let alone this guy's. So I didn't know what to make of it.

He treated Frankie well, I noticed. Very gentlemanly toward her. This had the charm of novelty to it, certainly, and her eyes were bright and flashing as she spoke. She usually takes to a rawer type. For the most part, they are men of diminished expectations, their only redeeming quality the ability to drink themselves senseless. Word has it she's crazy about making love but, unfortunately, is not very good at it. I didn't understand this business that came out later in the newspaper—the "platonic" relationship with the doctor. Maybe. But I doubt it, as she is hardly inviolable. One of my customers, who lives close to Frankie, observed her through her front window one night on top of some guy. Frankie had neglected to draw the blinds. He couldn't see the guy very well but said he would raise and lower one arm occasionally like a drowning victim.

If one may say so without irreverence, Frankie's face is not unattractive, even with that nose. This alone caused her, without her knowledge, to be made an honorary member of the local Liars Club. But the rest of her is rather burly. She's certainly not my type. I'm not sure what my type is anymore. I seem to have fallen into an off-category. But to get back on track. . . .

At about this point in the evening, I caught a curious exchange between the two, overheard as I was walking past them to hand an order to the cook. "You don't understand," Frankie was saying, "I am trying my utmost . . . but, *my health is within me,*" and, for emphasis, slapped her heart several times quite ardently. The doctor stared at her as if confronted by a complete dolt. "Well," he says, slapping the top of his head twice, "my hair is without me," and then about fell on the floor laughing about it. I just shook my head a little to clear it and walked on to the kitchen.

This had put him in a jocular mood, though, and soon afterwards, he told Frankie and me a joke. It's not worth repeating. I'd heard it years ago. Frankie, however, fell about laughing hilariously for a full minute. Customers turned to look at her, thinking, perhaps as I was: Time to cut her off. Barking was next up, and that, in front of her new beau, wouldn't do. I'm afraid I regarded the joke with little interest. "Aw, he's heard it!" the doctor exclaimed.

Bartenders are subject to hearing more jokes than anyone else in the world, and I'd heard this one in about 19 and 83 and, even then, found it bereft of wit. To make up for my having heard it, I guess, he then wanted to buy me a drink. But I don't drink anymore to speak of, and never at work. I used to drink at work but often found myself dancing with the dishrag late at night. I became then somewhat incoherent with the change I was handing out. Frankie went to the bathroom shortly thereafter. The doctor looked at me, smiled big, lifted one leg a bit and cut one that sounded like a trumpet being strangled. It all but propelled him off the stool. "Bet you never heard that one," he laughed.

Then he played a game of pool, was beaten quickly, and blamed it on the felt being rough. I think he lost five bucks to Red, or Blackie, one of our amateur pool sharks. They all seem to have names like that. Whitey was another one. I understand White's out of detox now and looks like hell. He quit drinking, but hardly soon enough—about 20 years late I should think. But the doctor returned from the tables and said very somberly to Frankie, "I did the best I could." His voice was kind of reedy saying it. I thought, What's he talking about? He broke the rack, nothing went in, and the game was over about two minutes later. He seemed to have expended much energy in the process, however, and came back mopping his brow with a bandanna handkerchief. His nose had gone a curious shade of violet and appeared to be pulsating like an electric sign. I simply noted to myself at the time that he was a likely candidate for a stroke.

Though I must admit, I hardly understand the ins and outs of longevity. Not so very long ago, Minnesota Fats passed away. He was 85. Here was a man who did little else in life but play pool for weeks at a time with no sleep, all the while smoking cigarettes and eating pickled pigs' feet. There's some question whether Minnesota Fats didn't talk a better game than he played, yet he would have made short shrift of our lot. They're not that good. You show them money, however, they'll break you usually. You can even be a decent player, but you play half-drunk there's nothing you can do. They've been waiting on you, and they're used to playing wasted.

Anyway, he and Frankie were here awhile, and then they left. I saw her kind of tidy him up. Straightened his collar a bit. He'd just played "I Only Have Eyes For You" by the Flamingoes (you see how up to date our selection is) on the jukebox and hadn't once looked her way. Then I had glasses to wash. I didn't see them leave.

The second time the doctor came to the bar was maybe a week later. He came in alone one late afternoon. This visit, it's like somebody'd pulled the plug on his eyes. They were drained. He appeared to be taking a standing 8-count. He glanced around the place in a sort of wonder, as if he didn't quite understand how he'd ended up here. I thought, I don't know why exactly, that he wanted to talk to me. Then, perhaps sensing a reticence on my part, the only thing he said was, "A draft." He picked up a newspaper somebody'd left on the bar, hid behind it, and the next time I thought about him, he was gone. He didn't even finish his beer, all but unheard of in this bar. But you see guys like that sometimes working through a bad one. Then they get a good night's sleep, things right themselves, they get up the next morning and have a drink, and they're all but brand new again. So I didn't think too much about it, until Frankie came in that same night.

She came in about 9:30, wearing a primrose yellow blouse and blue vinyl skirt, high heels. She has a predilection for black pantsuits normally. She had on perfume that smelled like geraniums. All dressed up, it struck me, like people dress up sometimes to make themselves feel better. She had been to another bar already or else got drunk at home, her eyes heavy-lidded. It was a slow night. I've been trying to cut down on my smoking. I set an ashtray at the very far end of the bar. I'll light a cigarette there, take a drag or two, leave it in the ashtray and go about my business. So it's not in my hand all the time, or close at hand, say. Frankie sat down by the ashtray, and when I'd go there throughout the night, we'd talk a little.

I mentioned that her fella had been in earlier. I thought maybe they had something big going between them, but she said, no, it wasn't so big. You discount any sort of irony when talking to Frankie; it's out of the picture. Then she, to herself I realized later, though she spoke aloud, said all but incredulously, "He shaves his back!" I thought she was talking to me and replied, "Well, there you have it," not knowing quite what to say to that.

In a later conversation by the ashtray, I mentioned how dismal he had looked that afternoon. Frankie said, "He has trouble with the winter solstice." As if that covered it, she put out her cigarette and left to go to the bathroom.

Ten minutes later, she revived the subject. "He tried to take himself out once on the solstice. Five years ago. Or six, maybe. Before he moved here." This was my first hint that he wasn't a tourist, but I didn't pursue it. You have to remember that, basically, I was just making small talk to pass the time. "When I first ran into him," Frankie went on, "I asked him where he was from. 'I came from Death,' he says. He's real dramatic like. He was an actor, you know. He could a been a star, too . . . but he stubbed his nose."

Frankie has her way with words.

He stubbed his nose. What in the world could that mean? Stubbed it on an enormous amount of gin I would say.

"He took some pills," she continued. "He was in a coma five days. You ever been in a coma, Ben?"

"No," I said, "but I know the feeling."

"He told me he was disappointed when he woke up."

"You ought to keep an eye on him," I said. "He looked bad this afternoon."

"Naw," Frankie said. "He's probably just hung over. There's no way he'd try that again. He's got too much going for him."

As is my way, I didn't ask what.

I asked her instead—I hadn't half enough considered what I was saying, it just came out—"He's not married is he?"

"No," Frankie said. "I don't go out with married men."

She looked at me. I just nodded my head several times slightly. I don't know exactly who she thought she was talking to.

"He's in love with someone, though. I don't know her. I ain't even sure she exists."

"Why do you say that?"

"Well . . . sometimes when he talks about her, she's alive. Then other times, she died awhile back. I think she's just someone fanciful," Frankie said. "That's what I want to think anyway." A moment later, she added, "It's a shame."

To lighten the mood a little I said, "He's a hell of a pool player, though."

She forced a smile, shaking her head *no.*

"Pool. The ponies. Cards. He lost in everything he done. He just could not have any luck."

A man up the bar raised his hand then, and I went to get him a beer. As I was doing so, I kept thinking that Frankie's boyfriend had indeed looked like the tail end of bad luck earlier in the day. But I didn't believe it had a thing to do with games of chance. When I glanced down toward Frankie again, it just looked like a mop on the bar. She was asleep. It was midnight.

I heard one other item about the doctor, just recently, from Arlin Weber, the town librarian. Arlin has a face that looks to have been knocked about like a nine-pin, with fretwork about his light-grey eyes and a twinkle within. Our library has a large endowment from the Barthle family, who own the paper mill, and for a small town library, it is quite modern and, to Arlin's credit, contains a decent selection of reading material. He is related to the Barthles; it is how things get done here. But he and I hold informal discussions on books once a month. We'll both read a certain book, then he'll come to the bar, usually on

Sunday evenings, which tend to be quiet, and we'll talk about it.

Does it surprise you that a bartender reads books? It shouldn't. This job, this life really, is a long engagement against boredom, and I take comfort in books. But Arlin tells me this:

"That doctor that killed himself . . . he used to be around the library sometimes. He was a character. Sort of picturesque. When we'd talk, it all seemed tongue-in-cheek with him . . . as if to say, *There's more to me than meets the eye.* He'd come in Saturday afternoons. Every other Saturday maybe . . . looking up information on the computer. Journal articles mostly. He worked at what he did, I think. Kind of a student. A learner. But he had another angle, too."

"How do you mean?"

"Well . . . it's like this . . . I watched him and saw him do it a couple times, and I didn't realize what he was up to till he did it to me. . . ."

"Go on," I said.

"What he'd do was . . . anybody squatted down in his vicinity, say to look at a selection on a lower shelf, he'd walk over to where they were and lay a little fart on their head. It was a . . . hobby of his, I guess you'd say. Just lay one on you about the size of a quail egg. Then he'd go about his business, like nothing had happened. Can you picture it? I mean . . . what a goof."

Craziness is a part-time amusement for some people and too important to abandon to science is what I say. Writing this some two months after the doctor's final act, I'm curious now as to what Frankie said that night, about his earlier suicide attempt. If he took pills, surely he would know the correct dose. You have to wonder if he really wanted it that time. Maybe he was uncertain then, only flirting. And I realize that, sometimes, when people make this decision, they are already very high and can't keep track. I must admit that I, too, have contemplated this act, perhaps as my retirement plan, though I've never been able to empty my mind enough to fit in the entire notion. Frankie, in the meanwhile, hasn't been back to the bar since the tragedy and seems to have disappeared from town.

And, of course, none of this, however odd, accounts for why the doctor killed himself. I wonder if that ever adds up, though? Maybe only to the one who leaves.

In Japan, the custom of *seppuka,* or stomach cutting—this had to do with a release of the inner person—supported an attitude that death must be faced squarely, with courage and tranquility. Death was regarded as one of the most important features of life, capable of playing a positive role. I have to compare this to some information I came across just yesterday, in the Tampa paper, about a former track star who tried to kill himself by drinking antifreeze. He regained consciousness a week later. When asked why he did it, he said: "I felt like I had no reason not to." Besides a lack of philosophy or system behind this effort, I was struck with horror by the thought of the incredible hangover that antifreeze must leave you with.

Everyone of us is such a separate mystery, incongruous even to ourselves much of the time. I, personally, have found little harmony to this life. It is more like a slow brawl. But I see that some people die with their eyes open and some with them closed.

When I was younger, I wanted very much to be a writer. I still keep a journal; it's all this is, really. An entry. I read books to take me out of this town that, in everyday life, I was never quite able to escape. If you ask me why the doctor killed himself, I can't be objective but must filter it through myself. Were you to accept it on that basis, here's what I believe: I think he was a man who made promises to himself and then didn't keep them.

A large black bear raided our Dumpster late Friday night. He seemed especially hungry. He sorted out the Dumpster. He licked the two outside barbecue grills clean. He came over and sniffed one of our inebriates who was sleeping by the back door, waking him. Though this fella is hardly a reliable witness, he reported that the bear was wildly drunk and acted all but affectionate toward him. Afterwards, the bear went three doors down and dug up an old lady's compost pile.

It brought to mind the doctor by some thread, and I began working on this. Otherwise, he has simply been forgotten, as thoroughly as though he never existed, and life moves as drowsily as ever in our town.

I still can't remember that word the doctor used—the one that gave him away.

It's floating somewhere here in the bar smoke. It'll come to me eventually. Most of them come to me sooner or later.

I Will Hide in God

Sunday night, the last day of March in 1968, the President went on television in the States and declared a unilateral cease fire along the DMZ. It meant that we could no longer fire into North Vietnam or the Demilitarized Zone, and when our Top Sergeant explained it to us, he was clearly disgusted. In addition to this, by the end of the week, the 101st Airborne broke the seige at Khe Sanh, and for the first time since I'd been in-country, some nights our guns were idle.

Camp Carroll was a big Marine base on a flat mountaintop along side the DMZ. We were Army, 175mm self-propelled artillery attached to the Marines. Our guns fired 14 miles. Each shell weighed 143 pounds. There were four guns to a battery. Three batteries on the hill.

Khe Sanh was 12 miles to the west. We'd fire there on whole grid squares at a time, using the time-on-target technique, in which all the rounds land and detonate at the same moment. As a rule, the guns took two sides of a secondary box. We'd deliver fire missions in long lines, 500 meters away from the primary box. Our fire rolled in toward the center and out again.

Anyone within a hundred meter radius of a single shell at point of impact was gone. But we never got to see the results. It was long-haul death, anonymous killing. The only time we were ever told anything was if we fucked up somehow. I was the #4 man on our crew, the triggerman. I did this job at night and humped ammo, too, and in the daytime I filled sandbags or pulled guard duty. I'd done it for nearly three months, had all but forgotten what sleep meant, and I, and everyone around me, was insane.

Now the NVA gave it back. They had many scores to settle, and each night they reminded us. What most concerned us were the Russian-made 122 rockets, as they had a delayed fuse and could penetrate our bunkers before detonating, rather than detonating on contact. Some of them were delayed and some weren't. But because of the delayed fuse, we feared them. They were serious weapons.

North Vietnam was in plain sight, the highest mountains in the distance, the DMZ mountains in front of them, and from these you'd hear the dull, far off *trump* as the rockets were launched. Route 9, our supply line from Dong Ha, was cut. This would change soon, but it hadn't yet. There was no mail. We had little news from the world and only rumors of what was happening directly around us. There were always many rumors. We were eating pancakes with grape jelly twice a day, C-rations once, and had grape Kool-aid to drink. Day in and day out. And a cold rain had started falling in the mountains.

That morning I'd seen my first live NVA soldiers. A patrol had captured them outside the perimeter, two little guys in black pajamas and tire thongs who squatted in the mud on the LZ not far from our mess tent. A chopper would come shortly and pick them up. Two grizzled Marines guarded them. One Marine said to the other, "What do you think?" The other Marine said, "I think I feel sorry for them." I, personally, didn't feel sorry for them. But neither did I hate them. What struck me most was that they appeared to be no more than children.

I went to the mess line and got in behind our Top Sergeant. "How would you like your pancakes this morning, Top?" one of the cooks asked. "Burn 'em, fuck 'em," Top answered. Exactly, I thought. And eloquently put. His disgust had rubbed off on us, and he was the only one in camp we looked to for leadership.

We had just recently acquired a new Battery Commander from the States. Few of us had actually seen him. He wouldn't come out of his bunker. The one time he was spotted in the open, he kept looking at the sky. We named him Chicken Little. The Captain before him had a pencil neck and a large head that seemed always to lay to one side or the other, as if it were to soon topple over. Which it did, finally, in a way. He suffered a complete nervous breakdown and was shipped to Japan. But it didn't matter who our officers were because Top ran the show. He was a mean son of a bitch, yet even his authority had eroded under the present conditions. Just no one gave a shit anymore.

We had grown nonchalant about the war. Since I had been in-country, even with all that we'd been through, through Tet and the siege of Khe Sanh, no one had been lost in our battery, and sometimes, if we weren't on the guns, my friends and I would sit on top of Communications, our tallest and most stalwart bunker, and watch the incoming like it was a fireworks display. We'd sit there and smoke and goof on the lifers. We'd talk about our hometowns, and hometown girls, about Saturday nights in an America that was, and what we were going to do when we got back to the world.

Then one night in early March, the Communications bunker took a direct hit by a 122. With the delayed fuse, it went right through the bunker, and Mosely and Alfredo Lopez, two of the guys I'd come over with, were killed. I was the first one in the bunker after that hit. Mosely was saying something and I thought he was okay, but the back of his head was missing. Alfredo was gone already and had the smallest death wound I would ever see. Just a little cut over his left eye. It was only big enough to let his soul pass.

That had been the start of it, and everything had been on a downhill slide ever since. Top soon had us doing all kinds of stateside bullshit during the day to keep us occupied and to instill discipline. Roll call in the mornings, policing the area. He even made us put polish on our boots, which was a farce because of the mud. Awhile back, his wife had sent him some rat poison from Ft. Sill. He set that out now, and there were rats popping up all over the place, gasping for air and dying at your feet. It was all but certain that we were now in some province of the Damned. There was little doubt left about that.

This particular day I'm speaking of, that evening at dark, me and this Puerto Rican buddy went looking for an empty bunker to have a smoke. The rain had stopped and the sky was clear but for some clouds that scudded along. The moon was lying on its back. The whole area was bunkers with sandbags piled on top and, in the moon and star light, resembled a small village of igloos.

My buddy's first name was José María. He was one of our truck mechanics. It was the first such name as that I'd ever come across, being from a small, German town in Ohio, where everything was more conventional and Lutheran. The name had quickly been shortened to Joey in the battery. He was a kid with a quick smile. He'd come in-country a month after I had. He'd put up a little statue of

St. Jude on top of his footlocker in our Quonset hut and every night faced it toward the incoming. I don't know if it was because of this or not, but nothing came down in our area. He'd spent all of one month at the foot of the cross, so to speak, but lately he'd started to loosen up.

After trying to talk to him several times early on, I realized he didn't speak English worth a damn, only a couple words and phrases, and he knew the curse words thoroughly. That was it. He knew his ganja well, though, and we had become friends. When he smoked he'd get to chattering away in Spanish. He'd talk to me in Spanish and I to him in American, and it didn't matter. We'd had many such conversations of late.

He was a terrific mechanic and had an obsession about fixing anything that was broken. This night he was working on a small, portable radio and carried it with him now.

Before we'd gotten very far, however, the rockets started falling. We ducked into the nearest bunker. Somebody had thrown up at the entrance. You could smell it. Joey shined his flashlight around. There was a grunt in there already, a Marine. He turned his face away from the light. He didn't say anything to us, but then he groaned.

"You alright?" I asked.

"Naw," he said. "I'm sick as a goddamn dog."

He had his poncho over him like a shawl.

"You did some pretty work back there," I said.

"Sorry," he said. "Least I didn't do it in here. I try to be polite like that."

The rockets were hitting to the east of us in the 105 howitzer sector, another Army unit.

Joey rigged his flashlight to his helmet like a miner's lamp and started working on the radio. It was the only light in there, and it shone dimly. The bunker was small. You couldn't stand up in it all the way. The ceiling was tree bamboo. On top of this, our long shell casings filled with sand, and sandbags over it all. One or two more men could have fit in comfortably. If Joey could get the radio going, it would be like the Ritz.

The only station we could pick up lately was Hanoi Hanna's. She played some decent music and her propaganda was good for a laugh. Earlier in the week she'd played a record by a singer named Janis Joplin. One of the new guys said, "No, she ain't black. She's white." But nobody believed him.

Joey took out a reef and lit it. I lit two and handed one to the Marine.

After awhile the Marine said, "That's some fine smoke, is what it amounts to." It came sealed in clear plastic, already rolled, ten to a pack. It was the one supply, besides ammunition, that always got through. It smelled of earth and mold and had many healing properties, one of which was to allow you to laugh in Hell.

Each time a rocket struck outside, the Marine started. In the faint light, he seemed no more than a live shadow. Sometimes you'd see his face a little when he dragged on a cigarette. He had a gunny sack at his feet. I was hoping it didn't contain his collection of ears or any similar trophies. Recently a necklace of small monkey skulls had been offered for purchase by a Marine who seemed slightly incoherent just then. It was very attractive, but I didn't feel like anything like that tonight. The rockets were intermittent now. Then another one struck.

"Motherfuckers," the Marine said. He had a broken voice. He croaked and rasped his words. He was with the 1/26 Marines. He'd just returned from one of the hills around Khe Sanh. He had malaria, the kind that comes back on you from time to time, and he had the flu.

"I'm better now," he said. "You should a seen me before. It was fucking grim."

The Marines were across the road from us. We didn't go over there, and they didn't come this way much. It didn't pay to make friends with Marines because you would soon lose them. But I was curious what he was doing over on our side and asked him about it.

He reached down and shook the bag.

"I got some beers," he said, "I want to trade for Cokes."

Many of the Marines were so young they'd not acquired a taste for beer.

"How many you have?"

"Seven," he said.

Another rocket hit. They were getting in toward us.

"We got no Cokes, no beer. We got shit," I said. "You wouldn't care to sell a couple them?"

"For what . . . money? What good is that? I went to you all's PX yesterday. I don't know why they keep it open. There ain't nothin' in the goddamn thing. I mean nothin'."

I said, "I don't go there only unless I have to."

Soon after I said this I was wondering what it meant. There'd never been anything in the PX since I'd been here. Then I realized the reef had snuck up on me. It brought me back to the point from which I had wandered, whatever that was, and just then the Marine said, "What?" and we all laughed.

I saw his arm motion toward Joey.

"He's workin' at it, ain't he?"

"I've never seen him tire at it," I said.

"Aw shit," he said, as another rocket hit. "That son of a bitch is walkin' right to us."

Joey had stopped his work and was listening. He'd picked it up, too. "*Coño,*" he said. Then he said some other things fast.

We heard another far *trump* in the mountains, and soon the incoming shrieked, a kind of metallic squeal, once heard, never forgotten, and, to us very much, one of the voices of Death. Then the detonation, this round 20 meters closer than the last and on a direct line walking toward us.

There were two, maybe three crews working in the mountains, though it was hard to be certain because of the distance, and that they moved around some. But this one was definitely working our grid and, just by the luck of that blind draw, had us in his sights. The next one came in closer. You could really hear it strike, and then the shrapnel whizzing around and hitting the sandbags up top.

I saw Joey cross himself, and he began to pray aloud in Spanish:

> "*Jehová es mi roca,*
> *mi fortaleza y mi salvador.*
> *Yo me esconderé en Dios,* *(I will hide in God)*
> *que es me roca y mi refugio. . . .*"

I lit a cigarette. And when Joey turned off his flashlight, I started praying, too. I had never prayed before in earnest, but only in church when they told you to. Over a quarter century has passed since that night, and I don't recall altogether what I said. But it was a very simple prayer and had to do with a desire to stay alive. There was a grunt proverb in Vietnam that went: *There's one bullet in this country with your name on it.* And I remember asking God, saying it inside myself and not aloud, "Let my name not be on this one."

Said that a couple times I think. And I finished by promising that I would do right from then on. It is something I've repeated a few times since over the years and never quite lived up to. Even then I was thinking—Maybe I shouldn't have said that last part.

Joey was still praying quietly in Spanish, and the Marine was saying, "You cocksucking son of a bitch," when we heard the rocket launched in the mountains. Then very soon it struck. I didn't hear this one coming. Nothing. It just hit and groaned quickly down through the center of the bunker. And you have to know these are just words. It all happened inside of no time at all. I felt heat. Then several seconds later, I came to.

I was coughing. I was taking in smoke and dust and not much air, and I realized that I was on top of the Marine.

He said, "Get off me will you goddamn it. I got my arm tangled under me here."

"Joey?" I said.

"Tomás!"

"What happened?" I said.

"It was a dud," the Marine said. "Let's get out a here, though."

Another rocket struck somewhere beyond us.

"Get the fuck out a here!" the Marine said.

Four men died on Carroll that night, and three others were lucky not to be counted. The round had penetrated the bunker, mangled the ceiling where it came through, passed down between the three of us and buried itself in the ground. Some demolition personnel dug it out the next morning and disposed of it.

Afterwards, I could never clearly recall that Marine's face. When we'd made our way out of the bunker, I heard him say in that broken voice: "Motherfucking bullshit country." And he vanished into the night.

The Star Train

We were coming back from Biarritz. We crossed into Spain and had a two hour wait at the station in Irun. We would have to switch trains. We went to the station restaurant. Jane ordered calamari. I started drinking beer. I was throwing them down, one after the other. And Jane began to level her eyes at me, as she knows from experience what this means—some act of lunacy is soon to follow.

But I was just steeling myself. We wouldn't be in Madrid until 7 am. It would be a long trip, and I knew already from the ticket agent that our train had no barcar, which I considered even more unfortunate. There are some fine trains in Spain, but ours wasn't one of them. We were taking an *estrella*, a Star Train. They are from another era. It's more akin to stagecoach travel or the freights they bring the fish in to the markets of Madrid. There is something hopelessly ramshackle in how they handle the tracks. Plus they pack you in. I could expect no comfort. No sleep. My thought was to get as drunk as possible and hope for the best. It was a plan I came up with often enough, and sometimes it even worked.

After awhile, I begin to notice two guys standing at the bar who had been in the restaurant long as we had. The shorter of the two, he's kind of built, black hair cut close, receding at the temples, has a day beard and a little beer gut. He's matching me on the drinks. The other is taller, thin, drinking not at all. These two would, by coincidence, end up in our coach this night.

We board finally, find our car, compartment. The whole train is second class, but in Spain you have to reserve your seat on long trips. There's an old couple in the compartment already—Fermin and Amelia. We get to talking. The conversation is a mixture of Spanish, French, and I find it somewhat confusing. But I understand that they left Spain during the Civil War and had lived in Paris ever since. They didn't stop back for visits until Franco was dead. Fermin's this little old gentleman, immaculately dressed, has a mischievious glint in his eyes, and a sweetness there caused by a life that has aged well. His wife is fully twice his size, gruff, a big talker. She was starting to work on my nerves, but I'd brought three bottles of Bordeaux along. After a couple hits on the first bottle, she changed for the better. She turned it around completely.

The compartment seats four comfortably. There's two small bunks up top, which are full of luggage already. I'm thinking maybe we lucked out. Just as soon as I think this, in comes two more, a young couple from Madrid. The fella speaks some English. They pile in. Still, it's not too bad—they're both skinny. However, right before the train departs, here come the two guys from the restaurant. Now, as the train starts moving, we're eight sardines.

Eight people are the makings of a party to me. I open the other two bottles of wine, pass them around. The taller fella is named Ouardi Hmidou. He's from Al-Hoceima in Morocco. Ouardi is a language teacher, fluent in English, Spanish, French and Arabic. So the language barrier is down. We can all talk to each other and know exactly what's going on. We have an interpreter. The other fella is named Roberto, a Madrileño. He'd brought along a bottle of *manzanilla.* Everyone's having a good time now, even though we're hopelessly crushed in there. This goes on for awhile, until the wine and sherry ran out, when I lost interest in the party entirely.

Years ago in Tampa I got stuck on an elevator that had suddenly gone mad without warning. I was in there with five, six others, shoulder to shoulder. The elevator would stop at a floor, whichever one it chose, but would do so wrongly. The doors would open. Either on the top or bottom, there'd be a space. It varied each time, two foot once, six inches the next, etc., where you could see people standing there waiting to get on. They'd wave; then the thing would take off again to its next randomly chosen destination. It went on and on. This was the birth of my claustrophobia.

So I left the party, stood out by the W.C.—stood there for hours, smoking.

About 2 a.m. this fella from our compartment, Roberto, comes and joins me. He'd passed out for awhile. He's talking to me in Spanish. It's high-speed Castellano, and I don't understand much. He's one of these guys likes to get up close; he's all but standing on my boots talking to me, thinks eye contact is an important item.

Finally he says, "*Es escritor?*" He'd heard me tell Fermin I was a writer.

"Sometimes," I said.

All of a sudden he says, "Charles Bukowski!"

Incredulous, I asked, "What? Wha'd you say?"

"Bukowski!"

Then he starts talking in English.

"I saw you in the restaurant," he says. "You were really putting them away."

"Yeah," I said. "I saw you, too."

He tells me he spent a year at M.I.T. in Mass. He's a physicist, he says. Maybe, I'm thinking. Who knows. People tell me shit all the time. Up till now I just thought he was a drunk. He never says anything more about Bukowski but tells me about this bar in Valladolid. It's a town about halfway to Madrid, and we'll be coming to it soon. The bar's a couple blocks from the train station. There's a layover. He says if we run there, we'll have 15 minutes, can get a cognac. There's a beautiful barmaid runs the place. He takes his ease with her from time to time. He's on this train a lot, he says, though I never find out why.

There's a giant yard at the Valladolid station. We jump from the train, it's raining a bit, cross over eight, nine sets of tracks, go through a hole in the fence, then two blocks to this corner bar.

He orders me a double cognac and a beer, gets a beer for himself. Orders this from the barmaid he'd been talking up. She hardly gives him the time of day—a peroxide blonde, 200 pounds, thick neck—and if anything, seems a bit put out to see him in her bar again.

I look at Roberto. We toast, clink beer bottles.

"Roberto . . ." I say. "I had a friend by that name once."

He says, "Henry Miller!"

I take a sip of cognac. Henry Miller. Only yesterday I'd been looking through *Black Spring* once more, "The Fourteenth Ward" and "Burlesk." I went with it.

"How's he do it?" I said. "He'll pack words like *coccyx, lysol, Honyhnhms, griddle-sizzle*—load 'em up in one sentence, an' somehow it works. There's this natural rhythm to the language, it's familiar (I take another sip of cognac), everyday, even . . . but the words are unexpected. It's like jazz."

He looked at me like I was a madman, ordered another beer.

I glance around the place. It's a dive, has a good feel to it. There are five large women here and there. The focus of the place seemed to be the payphone in the corner. They were all keeping an eye on it. It never rang. There's one petite, good-looking woman sitting at a booth with a black dog. She's sitting on one side of the table and the dog on the other. They're facing each other. I didn't even want to think too much on that one.

Roberto throws down another beer. Somehow, I'm thinking, I'm going to end up paying for all this, right? Easily foretold.

He orders another, looks at me, says, "Rimbaud!"

I say, "What d'you know about Rimbaud?"

He thinks for a moment or two, says, "Lorca!"

One of the fatsos comes over and asks for some *pesetas* for the jukebox. I give her a couple *cien*, feeling expansive. "What do you want to hear, Roberto?" I ask, even though the woman's already forgotten us.

He says, "Meatloaf!"

Meatloaf?

"You like Meatloaf?" he asks.

What do you say to that?

"He has that one song makes me laugh," I answer. "Where's he got that refrain where the woman says, 'Do you love me?' and he answers, 'Let me sleep on it.' Otherwise . . ." I trail off.

He thinks this over, shakes his head finally.

"I don't recall that one," he says.

There's a crone mopping the floor in the back toward the restrooms. She's somebody's granny. Roberto has just called out to her, got her attention. He waves, gives her a big smile. He says to me, "She's the barmaid's mother. I had her, too." The old lady deadpans him, goes back to her mopping.

We load up on as many beers as we can carry, hustle back to the train yard.

The train's gone.

I've got the money belt, passports, apartment keys. I can picture Jane. Even worse, I'm thinking I might have to spend the night with this lunatic. We chase around asking everyone we come across where the hell the train is. Finally a night watchman tells us the train hasn't left the yard yet. It had switched tracks, picked up some more cars. We find it.

We're standing outside the car, downing a couple more beers. There's a young Spanish guy off to our left about three feet, smoking a cigarette.

Roberto says, "I hate to go back in there."

"Me, too," I said. "Least we're in with some nice people."

"Who?"

"Fermin's a good guy. Him and his wife . . ." I don't get finished.

"The old people?" he says. "They're assholes."

He points to the young Spanish guy smoking there.

"See this guy? He's an asshole, too."

The young man says in perfect English: "No, I'm not an asshole. I just don't know English well enough to join the conversation."

The train starts up. I go back to my spot by the W.C., smoke endlessly, hours of it, leaning against the wall, the train rocking back and forth, catch a minute's sleep now and then, standing.

Near Avila the sky lightens. From Avila it's all downhill to Madrid. We'll be home in an hour and a half.

A gypsy comes back there, goes into the W.C. and smokes a *porro.* The hash smell follows him out. He lights a cigarette, looks out the windows at the dawn. He has long hair, dark half circles under his eyes. He's wearing the prettiest leather pants I've ever seen. Red-brown, shiny, handcrafted, it struck me, by someone who loved him very much—his mother, his sister. You couldn't buy anything like these are. His girlfriend comes out. She's got their backpacks. She's younger than he is by a good ten years. A tough face. Dressed in black linen, her complexion like bone china against it. She looks fresh, like she just took a bath. How do they do that?

The gypsy opens one of the packs and a little bullterrier steps out. One of those with the curved nose. He's black and white. He looks at them, wags his tail. He stretches in pure delight. Comes over and sniffs me. Dismisses me. He looks here and there, then runs around in a circle for awhile. Stops. Runs to the gypsy, pretends he's going to bite his boots.

At the Avila station, the gypsy snapped his fingers. The dog jumped into the pack. He was a gypsy dog—he knew how it worked.

The couple told me, "*Adios.*"

I asked in Spanish where they were headed.

"*La Calle de Muerte y Vida,*" she answered. The Street of Life and Death.

And they set off toward the walls of Avila.

Excerpts From

The Book Of Thieves

(from a novella called *Goya's Head)*

Not long ago, after a night I walked into the dawn, I came across a leprechaun shooting up in the tunnel under Paseo Recoletos, Plaza Colon. He had his works laid out there and was tightening a string on his arm. He said, "Jus' havin' me wee fix for the mornin'." Then he nickered like a horse. I was so surpised he spoke to me in Irish, I only shook my head a little to clear it, and walked on.

In restrospect, I understand I should have taken it for a sign. I wrote it off instead as just another Madrid street oddity. But soon afterwards I received a letter from Jack Putz.

He's going to school in a place called Port Muck, up near Belfast, the letter told me in a childish scrawl. Outside of the weather there, it sounded ideal: lodged in an old farm house by the sea, only 11 students; he's working on his Master's in poetry, and so on. Knowing Putz, though, I have an abiding suspicion there's something shady to it. He is purchasing a degree, say. He might be dropping by for the holidays, he tells me, if he can work it out. No return address. Signs his name Big Jack.

I was this boy's tutor several years ago in Florida. Trying to teach him how to write poetry was a forlorn endeavor. I'm thankful others now have the job. I'd like to know who gave him my address here. I'm pretty sure I didn't want him to have it.

My wife's friend, Sophie Veran, is an exchange student from Tampa. Her fiancé is coming over for the holidays, also. From some things Sophie's mentioned, Megan seems to think he's a black guy. This doesn't bother me. I don't get along with blacks any more than I don't get along with whites. Big Jack has me curious though. I can't remember him being so big. He was always writing poems about Vikings and Druids. He was lost in time like that, but neither was he working with any precise historical knowledge. His Vikings were perpetually landing on a shore in some unidentifiable country. They came at night in their longboats. Sometimes though, if I remember right, in one poem especially, I think they came in cars.

Wednesday morning: rain. The scene outside grainy as a 1920's movie. When it stops finally, a cloud descends into the streets. Widows move through this like black scarves in smoke.

Megan and I have rented a room at the *parador*, or state-run hotel, in the village of Sigüenza from the 24th to the 26th of December. It will be, I imagine, the only time we ever spend Christmas in a castle.

I receive two post cards from Big Jack Putz. The first one says: *Arrive the 23rd.* The second contained a short poem, about a Viking washing up on the shores of Madrid.

Then, as advertised, on the 23rd, just before noon, Big Jack arrived.

"Lucas . . . honey," Megan called to me. She was picking yellow leaves off the geraniums on the balcony. "There's a very large drunk boy with a red nose cursing at the buzzer." Our intercom is disconnected.

It was Jack. Looked like him in the face anyway. He has big teeth, with a gap between the two front ones. But he'd gained at least a hundred pounds since I'd seen him last. A wide 280 now, maybe more, and he's not but five seven in his boots. He was having a brief exchange with Nacho, one of our neighbors. He and his extended family own a Carbones shop down below. They sell cord wood and small pieces of coal. Jack had a flask he was nipping on.

We shake hands; then he goes to pay the taxi fare. He says to the cabby: "How many piñatas you need there, Ace?"

It takes a while to get him up the four flights of stairs. He's sweating his ass off, puffing and blowing. I'm wondering why he has so much luggage. He's staying two weeks it turns out.

"Wha'd you say to Nacho?"

"I said 'Fuck you too, ya goddamn ferret.' " Nacho has an unfortunate mustache that clearly places him in the weasel clan.

"What happened?"

"I flipped a cigar butt into his shop there. I wasn't looking. I thought it was an alley. He come out an' jumped in my face."

I introduce him to Megan. She takes an immediate dislike to him.

We install him in the extra bedroom. Within a half hour he turns it to a shambles. He unpacks, throws his clothes and papers around. The room looks like a debris area left by high water along a creek. He chews cigars until they resemble wet rats and then leaves them lying about for Megan to jump at. He's diabetic, and you come upon him at odd moments shooting up insulin. This recalls other times, other friends. It's disconcerting, until you remember exactly what he's doing. And he will simply fall asleep while you're talking to him. There are any number of people I felt might like to sleep during a conversation with me, but he's the first one to actually do it.

The diabetes does not stop him from eating pastry, however, and he will soon be frequenting the *churro* shop below. Or from drinking. He quickly downs every beer in the house—it wasn't even cold, a six of Aguila we had in the cupboard. No matter. He puts some clothes in the washer. Later, Megan hangs these up to dry in the building well. She calls me to the kitchen on some pretext, points out his drawers. She observes them in disbelief. They resemble a one-man camping tent.

She called Sophie to report this phenomenon. Her fiancé has arrived in town, and after awhile they come over. Her fiancé is this giant spade. He can barely get his shoulders through the doorway. His name is Erik Giles. He was an All-American swimmer at the University of Tampa a decade ago; I remember reading about him. Now he works for a health club in Palm Harbor, and he's obviously been using the facilities.

They, along with Sophie's lunatic roommate, June, have rented a place for New Year's Eve at the American Hostal, which overlooks Puerta del Sol. They invite us to come.

They'd brought along five bottles of wine, and we sit around and bullshit the rest of the afternoon. Erik can put it away. He drinks with the best of them. He manhandled two of the bottles himself. Putz recharges his glass often enough, but he gets a little maudlin in the process. He needs to call his girlfriend back in Tampa he says. Talks with her awhile. I take it things aren't going so well between them. After Sophie and Erik leave, Putz starts throwing up. He'd eaten everything we had in the icebox. It goes for naught.

After he'd regained his composure a bit, he asked me if I'd look over some of his poems.

"You're my mentor, Luke . . . you're the greatest!" This is said in a baying slur. "Are you working on anything?"

"A story," I say. "Maybe I'll put you in it."

"What's it called?"

"'Excerpts From The Book Of Thieves.'"

"What a title! That's terrific, Luke. I wish I could come up with something like that."

He went into the bedroom to get his poems and, luckily, didn't return. He passed out.

Megan is noticeably pissed.

"How old is he?" she asks.

"Twenty-two."

"When he drinks," she says, "he's only 13."

I'd have to agree, but I know the cause of it. His old man is a preacher. At least on Sundays. The rest of the week he trades in baseball cards. Both parents have sheltered him, especially his mother, who is a friend of mine, and a fine woman. But Ireland is the first time he's lived away from their influence. He was a teetotaler at home. In the upcoming days, he's going to share some scenes with us that he should have worked out with his buddies when he was a kid.

"He needs to learn how to drink," Megan says. She'd just finished cleaning the bathroom. "Look at this." She's pointing to one of Putz' cigars. He's laid this one to rest on her crossword puzzle. It sits there like some ravaged lizard.

"We're leaving for Siqüenza in the morning," I remind her.

"Thankfully," she says. "I can't take much more of this asshole."

I look at the clock. Putz has been in Madrid all of five hours.

For the sake of brevity, I'm afraid I can't take you to Sigüenza. Let me mention that the full moon docked at a castle parapet just beyond our balcony Christmas Eve, that they were days of luxury and romance in a lovely medieval town. But since the story isn't otherwise concerned with this place, it must suffice to say that we went there for some peace and quiet, so that worked out well; and it was certainly to be the last of that for awhile.

When we returned to Madrid, both the apartment and Putz were a complete mess. His girlfriend had called Christmas Day and given him some Dear John news. He's devastated. He's in ruins. He drank all the liquor in the house and then spent the rest of his money buying more. He's broke. He had mentioned several times being on a tight budget. Come to find out, he only brought a hundred bucks with him. And he can't go back to Ireland until the 5th of January. He'd eaten all the food in the house. We had gone shopping before we left. Now there's not even any sugar left, nothing. He ate the flour somehow. The place looks like it's been tossed by the cops. Megan's ready to throw him out on the street.

From now and until the time of Jack's departure on the 5th, Megan will assume a glacial air around him, which he never quite seems to notice.

She starts withdrawing large sums of money from the bank, giving it to me, telling me to go drink. Anything to get Putz out of the house. So Jack and I and Erik end up touring the bars. Madrid is a town built to an alcoholic's blueprint, and there's no end to the tour sites. We call it touching up the day. We make up strange plans to amuse ourselves, like doing some caroling in the neighborhood. Go around to the balconies, sing "We Three Kings," though we can't exactly remember the words. Day after day of this. I'm getting worn out. Putz is drinking his troubles away. He gets stumbling drunk, and he's a load to steer around in this condition.

He seems to have grown even larger since he arrived. He really gets into the *tapas.* Olives, *albóndigas*, cheese, shrimps, *calamares, chorizo*, ham, *morcilla,* clams. He shovels it down. He even likes *callos,* which is tripe. At one place they give him some barbecued pig ears. "Hey, Luke," he says, "look, there's hair on this shit. What is it?" I'm not interested in telling him. You don't know how he'll react. He'd already decorated several taverns in the neighborhood. We have to keep track of those we shouldn't return to.

One day, Megan and I and Putz go for lunch at the restaurant across the street from our apartment. *Platos combinados* are *750-900 pesetas,* the *Menú,* or daily special, 950. The food is cheap, they have a good waitress, nice checkered tablecloths, and it's a greasy spoon. As if to emphasize the point, whatever you ordered, the cook threw a fried egg on top of it. Megan had a meatball dish, I had roast pork, and Putz had fried fish. In an oddity of presentation I'd never quite seen before, they all appeared to be the same item.

Even stranger was the entertainment.

Putz ate two bites of his food and said he had to take a dump. He got up and left the table. I'm sitting there watching my plate coagulate, when in came 6-7 deaf and mute folks. They were that and also acted somewhat goofy. They're all dressed the same, hospital greens. I never did discover who their attendant was. Maybe he was out parking the van. Three of them, three ladies, had to go to the bathroom, and pretty bad, apparently. Lucky like that how we are, our table is located right next to the toilets.

The women's toilet is out of order. It's closed up, there's a sawhorse in front of it. And the men's toilet is locked from the inside, as Putz is now in there occupying it.

The three "signers" seemed to utterly flip over this locked door. Perhaps it was the sawhorse, too, inspired some ancient terror—I just couldn't understand it. But suddenly they're demented. One of them grabs the doorknob and starts yanking hell out of it. The second beats on the wall with her little fists. The third, the biggest of the lot, stands behind these two, admiring their work I took it, and from time to time, hops up and down wildly, although, bless her, she's kind of hefty and never quite gets off the ground.

I hear Putz say, "Hey, Luke . . . is that you? Quit foolin' around now." But the ladies are nearly routing the door, and it finally dawns on him that it's not me. He starts yelling, "Hey Motherfucker I'm Takin' A Shit Here Goddamn It!" The ladies, of course, can't hear this. Now from behind here comes the big one, rams the door with her shoulder. . . .

Putz is a weird looking character. He appears to be dressed in prison clothes. They fit him like sackcloth. His pants land in a puddle over his boots. No neck. Bristly head. I give him my watchcap to wear, and he pulls it down over his ears. He has a long winter coat he calls his Viking apparel, claims it's made of musk ox hide. He walks hunched over, headlong, but somehow as if he's in deep mud, gravity tugging heavily on him. He snorts and moans. It's like walking around town with a short bear.

All the time now he's crying in his beer over this girlfriend who dropped him. Her name is Pattie. She works in a fast food joint in Tampa. She went sweet on one of her fellow hamburger flippers. I've met this girl. A big blonde. A big body anyway; her head's kind of little. As far as I'm concerned, even Putz could do better. I finally tell him, "You mention Pattie's name in front of me one more time, I'm never going to speak to you again in my life."

The next morning he starts off, "Luke . . . you know that person I'm not supposed to mention no more?" And starts carrying on about her again. He just doesn't say her name.

One day he asked me to take a look at a poem he'd started since he came to Madrid. I'm expecting more Vikings, maybe some Druids. But it's even more appalling. The first three lines read like so:

I remember the apartment we had/it was over the police department/where you cooked me noodles. . . .

"What do you think?" he asked.

One of the oddest things was that he never strayed more than about a foot away from me. Try that sometime. After awhile it got so I'd just push him away, keep him at arm's length at least. Tell him, "Stay the fuck over there. What's the matter with you?" And he took little note of the many young women in the neighborhood. The university is nearby, 130,000 students. He couldn't see them through his sorrow I guess. Nor did it occur to him to go anywhere on his own. He'd just sit around in the evenings with Megan and me, like one of the old folks.

I started sending him to the market for wine. It allowed us a small measure of solitude. The old ladies there, however, are crazy in the check-out lines—you just can't let them share their madness with you—and they soon got the best of him. He returned one night empty-handed. He gave a short but impassioned speech: "It's brutal in the lines. I'm tired of being bullied by tiny, 80-year-old women. I've had it. I'm at the end of my rope. I'm starting to push back. They're stronger than they look. They're savage. I can't match them there. And stupid. I could use wit against them, but they wouldn't get it. They don't understand a goddamn thing I say. I'm thinking about dropping one with a right cross. Maybe the word will get around. They'd better watch their P's & Q's from now on, if you know what I mean."

It was like some nutter addressing the public at large. Noticing that he had stunned his immediate audience, he turned on his heels and went to bed.

I asked Megan, "Do you have any idea what that was all about? Try not to be uncharitable."

"Where's the wine?" she answered.

I find out some days later the old ladies had so unnerved him that he bolted from the store.

Finally, Megan tells him point blank one night, "You need to go out on your own tomorrow. I want to spend some time with Lucas."

He slaps himself in the temple. "That's just what I was thinking," he said. "That was just the thought I had in my mind."

Megan about rolls her eyes out of her head.

I give him 20 bucks in *pesetas,* and the next day he goes off by himself. That evening he doesn't say where he's been, but he's much happier. A big goofy smile. He's sort of manic.

Finally I asked him, "Wha'd you do today?"

The three of us were sitting in the livingroom.

"I went to a convent," he says.

"A convent?"

"It was really interesting. They have . . . like a trophy room."

"Relics," I said.

"Yeah. That's it. I saw St. Anthony of Padua's skull. He was the first one who read books without moving his lips. He sort of invented that." Putz glances at Megan, who is ignoring him, looks back and gives me a big wink.

He takes me aside at some point later.

"Luke," he says. "I think I fell in love."

Right off it comes to me—she has to be a replica of Pattie. A dead ringer.

"I want you to meet her," he says.

"When?"

"How 'bout now? It's early."

I figure he's out of money again and could use a drink. Anyway, we go downtown. As it turns out, he hasn't actually met the woman either. Would I introduce them? We end up on Calle Valverde. Whores and cops in equal number tonight. They stand around chatting with each other. There's live sex acts. Putz guides me along like I'm new in town, pointing out those parts of the street where was the most sport. He stops in front of a sex parlor.

"I'm gonna put you next to something good," he says.

He pretends like he's holding me back.

"Don't you run in there like a blind dog in a meat market now!" he says. He's laughing, getting a kick out of it. I remember in Florida he had this weakness for local color.

I went into a stall. Putz took the one next to me. He has some trouble with the lock on his door. He's banging it. The set-up is like a peep show, only when the window opens, there's live people there, young, sexual athletes presumably. At the moment, however, there's a woman lying on her stomach not even moving.

She's talking to her partner, who's behind the curtains. We're looking at the back of her head. A straw-haired blonde. Her ass looks like it's been deflated.

"Is that her?"

"I'm not sure," he says. "I can't see her face."

I hear him flopping around over there.

"Watch it, Luke," he says. "The floor's slippery."

There's a pane of glass between me and the woman. Somebody in there before seems to have pressed his whole face to the window. It's so smudged I can barely see. The pervert. She turns her body a little so I can see her cunt, shaved of course; it seems to be the vogue—all but for a little patch at the top that looks very much like Hitler's mustache. It must call to mind some strange thoughts dining there. She slaps it a couple times, maybe trying to wake it up. Putz starts yelling, "Hey, goddam, let's get with it!" Finally she notices that customers have arrived. She turns her face toward us and licks her shoulder—she's got the same little brush under her nose. It looks real. It's no five o'clock shadow. Maybe it's pasted on. That's got to be it. A stage prop. It's theatrical. All this runs through my mind in a moment. But I'll tell you, it made you feel like a goosestep or two right there, only there's not enough room.

"Definitely not the one," I hear Putz say.

I come out of the stall. Putz can't get the door open on his. He's locked in. He starts bellowing. I went outside the shop and had a smoke. He'd done the same thing at the apartment. Everything he touched broke. The hot water heater. The floor lamp. At the moment they're useless because he handled them. By the time I'm done with the cigarette, they've got him free.

He says not a word about being detained inside. He muses: "Nothing quite like a mustacheo'd woman."

We're walking aimlessly and soon cross the path of a tall transvestite. As we pass by, Putz gooses her. She starts following us shouting in English: "That'll be five bucks, pal . . . you owe me five bucks for that!"

We escape into the nearest bar. There are dancers on a catwalk. Others working the crowd. I wandered around, somewhat unsuccessfully, trying to find one that was acceptable to look at. They were all very large, naked—in truth, these bodies cried out for clothes—and bottle blonde, their hair in various stages of distress. The place was big, and I managed to lose Putz somehow. All of a sudden he wasn't beside me, and I didn't look very hard for him. I got a beer and found my way to the backroom, where the music wasn't so loud, and a sex show was just beginning—a fat lady and a midget.

The midget was this little old bald guy. He sported a handlebar mustache, had on combat boots, and that was it. He stood around doing muscle poses—which, he didn't exactly have any muscles to speak of, so it was pretty funny. He had to get up on a chair to reach the fat lady. She was enormous, her breasts like balloons that hung down below her waist.

It seemed more of a comedy routine than anything. She was so fat, he couldn't get to it. Finally he's trying to stick it in her arm, her ear, etc. And I guess it was part of the act, but they didn't seem to be on the best of terms. It looked to me that the fat lady wasn't pleased with this little guy for some reason. He was sort of stealing the show with his muscle poses, too. He was bringing down the house with that. Whenever he started this, she'd give him a homicidal look, which he totally ignored. Though, to my way of thinking, she didn't appear to be one you should cross. At this point, he pinched her or something, I missed exactly what happened. But she took one of her tits in her hand like a club and smashed him upside the head with it. He'd been into a muscle pose just then and didn't see it coming. He dropped off the chair like he'd been shot.

Freaks have always interested me. They are what a good many people look like, I suspect, if somehow a picture could be taken on the inside. They were just unlucky enough to be born without camouflage.

I'm thinking this when Putz reappeared at my side.

"Is he hurt?" he asked.

The backroom boys that had taken in the show are in stitches, but I'm keeping an eye on the midget. He hit the floor awkwardly and looks to have been coldcocked to me, but then again I'm not sure if it's part of the act or what. Before I can answer, Putz takes me by the arm.

"Come on," he says. We go back out front. He escorts me to one side. In the darkest corner, a man in a wheelchair was parked next to a dancer with ash blonde hair. He had on a 1930's hat tilted back on his head and held up a burned-out cigar as if making some point with it, but what struck me was the madcap expression on his face. He looked completely daft, like he was in a trance. Then I noticed one of the woman's hands was missing, sunk in his fly.

"That's her," Putz says.

Every morning now, Jack fries up a half dozen eggs in a pool of butter. The apartment is rancid with it. He can't bother with a plate. The frying pan is more direct. He wraps a dish towel around the handle, walks about the apartment with this and a fork, composing lines for his poem. We get to hear him think out loud, which is sort of frightening. He doesn't eat the food exactly; he inhales it. The toilet's on its last legs. It rocks back and forth now when you sit on it. The washing machine has learned how to walk. It apparently wants to escape. At night in bed, he snores loudly and has a varied repertoire of sleeping sounds. Bear snuffles. Seal barks. A duck gagging. We've got a zoo in there. Megan has taken to crossing off days on the calendar. The 5th of January has a big star by it.

New Year's Eve Day. Erik is here and our endless houseguest, who woke at noon, shot up insulin, then had some *churros* and a beer. We stay around the apartment all afternoon while Megan and Sophie are out shopping. Everyone's tired. The drinking excursions have taken their toll. Putz is completely strung out. The previous night, the three of us went down to the Lavapiés barrio looking for Cochran, this Irish friend, who wasn't around. We end up at Cafe Barbieri. At midnight Putz says he has to go home. He's bouncing from this to that, customers, tables, to and fro. He'd learned how to drink in Ireland he said, but not well we thought. He plows through the crowd. He gets to an area near the door where there's some couples dancing, stops and does some movements, like he's setting the hook on a fish—combined with this he appearred to be stamping out a cigarette with his right foot. I guess it was a dance step. Then he continued on. The metro's visible from the front door. Hard to miss. It's going to take him three hours to get back to the apartment, but we don't know this at the time. We don't even say goodbye. We just watch him leave. Erik said, "There goes Cinderella."

Erik calls his brother in the States. He puts down some bets on the bowl games. He's interesting to talk to. He's bright, irreverent. His hair is cut close to his big cat head. As big as he is, I notice he has a completely gentle manner with Sophie. He feels somewhat off base being away from his big screen TV, the sports channels. A while later, he called his brother again and upped the bet on Florida State. In my shirt pocket I find a napkin I'd written on last night in the bar. It says: *All looked have did badly, but the truth is knowing ever.*

It strikes me that, before Erik, I'd not had any sort of extended conversation with an American black man since Vietnam. More than a quarter century, that is to say. This place entered the conversation one day. Erik lost two uncles there. When he says this, we look at each other and don't talk about it anymore. There are not many blacks in Madrid and certainly very few as large as he is. He's sort of an attraction around the neighborhood. The entire Carbones crew seems petrified of him. When the three of us go into a bar around here now, it's an event. Nobody knows quite what to make of it, or what to expect.

Megan and I have rented a room in the Reina Victoria Hotel at Plaza Santa Ana for New Year's Eve. We go there around six. Our windows look out on the Plaza del Angel side. Across the street is Cafe Central. Bullfighters used to stay at this hotel in the old days. It wasn't so fancy back then, but neither were they. The most valorous now are no less than movie stars. At the same time, it's the only profession that requires you to wear pink socks, a sherbet-colored suit, and get covered in bull snot and blood when you work.

There are elegant people around the hotel lobby. I hear English, German, French, Portugese. Each group looks upon the others as if they're from a developing country. There's a lot of gold in the room. There are dark tans—these stand out in the Madrid winter. Most of the fellas are in tailored suits yet retain somehow the look of traveling salesmen. But the women are looking smart, no doubt about it. Some of their handbags must go for half a grand. Galliano is big with them. Stella McCartney. How do I know this? a man who buys exclusively from thrift shops. I overheard a conversation between two British ladies. They were quite critical of the room: "Check out the bitch in that muddy plum sort of thing. What would you call that look . . . chronic malaise?" And there are a few in lingerie-inspired silk dresses; these women appear to be wearing their slips. The old Spanish men from the neighborhood who drink at the bar observe them with some amusement.

There's something deeply superficial about this kind of rich, but they always look so good. The men could dress in white if they wanted and get away with it, whereas I should have such an outfit trashed within hours. I know farmers and ranchers from the interior of Florida who have as much money, but you'd never know it. They always look like they're going fishing.

The hotel room is larger than our entire apartment. We took two bottles of rioja with us, Castillo Ygay, black olives, Manchego cheese. We finished one bottle and went out for dinner. There's a little restaurant around the corner we eat at sometimes, most of its customers in the blue coveralls of the Madrid working man. The food is good and inexpensive. It was closed, however, and we ended up at a paella place on Echegaray. They had already run out of paella, but I wasn't so hungry anyway. I had a bowl of fish soup. It was neither bad nor good; it was of no consequence. I didn't pay attention to the price when I ordered. Megan had roast veal, which resembled jerky. When the bill came, my soup was 2300 *pesetas.* A place like that, you feel like they just stuck a hand in your pocket. Why bother to eat? I'm thinking. Just go to the door and throw cash at them. In my usual sage manner, I commented to Megan as we were leaving, "It should, at least, be the last indignity this particular year can hand us."

Around 10:30, in a pouring rain, we walked over to Puerta del Sol and the American Hostal. At Sol, ten streets meet and "debouch," as one old writer had it. The room is on the third floor. It's not a room for any of us to stay the night in; it is just to take in the scene. There's a balcony, all but too narrow to stand on. The room is small to begin with, and a bed takes up a good half of it. A bathroom with a shower. If you sit on the toilet, your head's lodged in the sink. There's Megan and I, Sophie and Erik, June Bug, Putz, and a Brazilian couple, Guillerme and Virginia, who take a Spanish class with Sophie. Virginia came to Madrid to learn the language. She's a real sweetheart, and her body just sort of knocks you backward. Guillerme is a lawyer in Rio, but he soon followed her. "How come?"

I asked. He speaks some English. He says, "Because of the way men look at her." I laugh awkwardly, I start looking around for something. Putz' theme for the night is to get "mortal drunk." He's going to "yodel in the thundermug," he says. We don't know what that means exactly, but we're to find out.

I'd given him some money the day before. With the last of that, he's purchased three bottles of very questionable wine, the cheapest he could find at the market. It's little more than swill. He drinks it out of the bottle, and he's not wasting time. He's doing some trying-to-forget kind of drinking. The bed is stacked with coats, beer, wine, cider, food. Not everyone can fit in the room at once. June Bug is saying how she had to pull strings to get it. We need to be on our best behavior, she keeps reminding us.

June always strikes me as a grown-up majorette. She threw her baton into the air one day, and it never came down. Life's been a little off since. Something missing. The big baton I take it. And *since* is getting on to ten years now. She and Sophie became roommates by circumstance and necessity, and it's been a mistake. Sophie was born in Paris, grew up in New York City. She's cool, lanky, 27. She has light-brown hair streaked with blonde that falls to the middle of her back, and tonight is dressed all in black leather. To her looks she adds vitality and good humor. Sophie is many things, in other words, that June Bug is not. The latter has chosen for the occasion a black and white pantsuit. The rest of the night, on the periphery of my vision, I'll be picking up a very large and dishevelled magpie or penguin. The pattern of the outfit seems to make her hips even wider, I notice, though they are hardly in need of exaggeration. She keeps close tabs on her possessions in their flat. She's told Sophie expressly not to let Erik use certain things. Especially don't use her soap she warned. Erik tells me he soaped up his ass good with that.

June Bug talks in a whine that drives me nuts. She needs someone to hand her a laugh certainly. Both she and Putz are so lame, I'm thinking something might shape up between them. I see them sitting together once. Before long Putz says, "Well . . . S C E U S E me," and shortly thereafter takes a nap while she's speaking to him. Down the hall a bit, there's a bar with a dance floor and a big long balcony that faces Sol; and out in the street there's 10,000 bedlamites in the downpour partying away.

Somewhere during the night I hear Putz ask Megan, "Why do his old friends in Tampa call him St.Luke?"

Megan answers, "The only thing saintly about Lucas is that he used to be so much worse." As things play out, this is to be the last complete sentence she ever says to him.

Close to midnight we're all out in the bar area, 15-20 people besides us, a good many of them American, the rest Spanish, just having a great time, but then, out of the corner of my eye, I notice a large penguin approaching me. I'm close to the balcony watching the crowd below, the sort of incredible number of umbrellas. At each gong of the bell across the street, the Spanish girl beside me has eaten a grape. She will eat twelve of them, for luck, she has just explained. June Bug whines, "J a c k n e e d s h e l p." I had an all but irresistable urge to knock the shit out of her. But outside they're counting down: *Seis. . . cinco. . . cuatro. . .* I look behind me. Putz is on the couch turning green. He's pickled.

Just then the New Year hit, but through the noise I hear a familiar gagging sound. Putz starts projectile vomiting. People around him are going, "Oh, for Christ's sake!" A nice older couple from Iowa, who were visiting their daughter in Madrid and that I'd had a pleasant conversation with earlier, are standing there with their hands limply outstretched, looking down at themselves in revulsion.

It took Guillerme, who doesn't even know the ass, the next hour to get him sober enough to put to bed. Holding his head under the cold water shower and all. He was flopping around like a fish. Finally he went comotose. We thought he might be dead, but nobody seemed overly concerned about it. Erik and I had to carry him from the bathroom to the bed; this was very much like trying to move a large pudding. We left him at the hostel to sleep it off. Megan says she has some cautionary advice for future visitors: Bring a lot of money and don't plan on staying long. And no children allowed.

But let me return to the street scene a moment. The craziness there had just kept getting rowdier. At midnight thousands of people uncork cava or champagne, make a toast, drink, then take the bottle by the throat, shake it and spray those standing around them. I saw an area down to the left that started clearing of people. There's an empty circle of cobblestones. I couldn't figure out why. All of a sudden the first bottle came flying out of the crowd and broke there. There's fireworks, bells tolling, everyone screaming and laughing, people thrashing around in the fountains, the statues covered with riders, all kind of noise-makers going, but here comes a hundred bottles breaking, now a thousand, and suddenly the scene turned into a cross between a celebration and riot. This went on until the whole plaza emptied of people. Nothing left but broken glass and police and the rain.

We returned to our hotel by 2 a.m. The next day at noon, back in our neighborhood, there were revelers still wandering around in tuxedos and evening dresses, champagne glasses in hand.

Putz showed up at the apartment soon after us. They found him in bed at the hostal and quickly gave him the boot. His clothes are still soaked. He's got hangover eyes like I've never seen before. They are orange and totally uninhabited. Somewhere into the third bottle of wine he lost track of the night. He doesn't remember it. He's curious why Megan refuses to speak to him.

Megan tells me, "I don't know who I'd rather have visit than Jack . . . though, any of the major root crops would have been fine. An artichoke even, or a nice leek would have sufficed."

There was snow in Madrid on New Year's afternoon, and it really came down—the Madrileños walking the streets under snow-covered umbrellas, the tree branches like Japanese prints. It covered everything, and I'd never seen the town prettier.

The 5th of January. This date had assumed the properties of a magic number. Coming back on the bus from the airport after seeing off Putz, I remember a dream I had in the night. I had shaved my beard and looked like someone else. I noted, as in all of my dreams lately, that I carried a loaded .38.

I'm not sure what it is about me—why the lame and bedeviled and those on a fool's errand gather to me like some mad constellation. It has always been this way. There is no end to their names, except when I forget them. Big Jack Putz is only the most recent. Maybe the bus was full of them even as I thought this. I didn't want to look around or notice it too clearly, but they stretch away from here on back through time.

I've never exactly determined my motivation for putting up with them. They have a certain entertainment value. They show me what I have fallen away from, perhaps. But it's something more that I don't understand. I have this notion they have stolen from me when they leave, though it's not something that's been inventoried, I can't say how much has been taken.

Our last bit of conversation, just before he boarded the plane, Putz tells me: "I come up with a good title for my poem."

I nodded vaguely.

"I'm gonna call it 'The Noodle Eaters,' " he said. "It's sort of like Van Gogh's 'The Potato Eaters,' see . . . only this is noodle eaters."

He'd been working hard on the poem the last couple nights. It's at 35 lines, few of which make the least bit of sense or seem in any way connected to the rest. It wasn't even poetry really. It was bad prose broken into lines so as to resemble a poem.

"You don't think it gives it away too much, though?" he asked.

The Drinking of Spirits

When I was a kid, I lived across the street from this church. It's maybe not the kind of church you're thinking of or the kind of neighborhood either. The congregation was small, 25, 30 at most. They would hold meetings on Wednesday night as well as on Sunday, and the women wore black lace veils. The church building had once been a hardware store, and it didn't look like much. Nobody in the neighborhood went to that church or really had a thing to do with it, the congregation came from other locations, and, consequently, say Wednesday evening, all the parking places on our part of the block would be taken. This didn't tally well with me and my buddies, because we'd play baseball there on the street, and it made the game kind of narrow.

We'd play anyway. Hit the red car, you got a double, and so on. The preacher's car was a home run because he was wise to us and would get down there first and park way on the corner. You'd really have to nail one to reach it.

It was said that this preacher handled snakes, but it was a mean neighborhood, and maybe this was only one of the jokes it told.

Next to the church was a basement house, which meant back then that someone with the best intentions had started to build a house, but had run short of cash. All that got done was the basement; after awhile the flat roof would be tarred, and that's how it stayed.

There was a widow lived in that house. Her name was Mrs. Hall. Even as little as I was then, I don't ever recall her being very big. And I liked her for that. That even though she was old, she hadn't ever grown up like everyone else.

She was poor, an old hillbilly woman who was in the habit of talking to herself, her hair like white iron, and, far as I could tell, she had only one passion in life and that was reading the newspaper.

My Dad told me much later than this particular summer I'm speaking of that she was related to us by marriage. She had come up from West Virginia as a mail-order bride around the time of the 1st World War to marry one of my grandmother's cousins, whose true love was rye whiskey. He was killed in an industrial accident at the Morton Salt Co. mine in Rittman. She got some settlement money from this, which a lawyer sagely convinced her to invest in coal stocks. Her husband had died so long ago, Dad didn't remember him well. And Mrs.Hall had worn black going on thirty years.

But like I say, she loved to read the newspaper, and Dad would save the *Cleveland Plain Dealer* each day so Mrs. Hall could come by the next day to get it. He would leave it in the garage. It was so she wouldn't ever have to ask him for it. Because she didn't care to deal with just everyone. The garage wasn't nothing you could park a car in. A long time back it had grown inward from the walls. There were things in there that, if they ever did have a purpose, had long ago lost it.

I played in the garage a lot—I had made a loft in there and it was sort of my headquarters—and I'd run into Mrs. Hall most every day. I thought she was a fine person, really, because when I'd catch frogs and crawfish in the crick that ran behind her house, she would buy them from me. It took me some time to realize she was probably eating the damn things. She'd give me the pennies she had around. Sometimes a nickel in among them.

She never spoke to my brother, Wade, who was three years older than me; as I said, she was eccentric in her friendships. And I never thought much about why she turned whatever good nature she had in her upon me. Though it strikes me now that I was probably the same age she was the last time she had known happiness. But she'd address the both of us sometimes: "I seen you boys throwin' stones at the church last night. You shouldn't ought to do that whenst they're a-meetin'," she'd say. "You'd better be careful. Pretty soon they'll be prayin' to send y'all to Hell." This would make absolutely no impression on us, other than to note that it was an awfully long speech for her.

In the summer, she'd know all the baseball scores. She was a fan of Rocky

Colovito and the Cleveland Indians. Cleveland was only thirty miles north of us, though at the time I had not yet been there. Colovito played right field for the Indians then, and he had a great arm. He could field a ball out near the fence, and, say he needed to throw home then, he'd damn near hit a strike to the catcher. I'd seen this happen on TV. At bat, he'd either strike out or hit a home run. There was nothing in-between about him. And his baseball card was a thing of real value in the neighborhood. It made you feel like you had cash in your pocket.

Mrs. Hall would come to get the paper, but since it was yesterday's, I'd be one up on her. She wouldn't ask right off who won the previous day. She'd say, "Give me the score." A little later, she'd ask for the name of the pitcher who got the decision. Then she'd know if the Indians won or not. She was always cagey about it, asked the questions sort of off hand, like the information wasn't of so much interest to her. If they lost, however, she'd walk away just a-cussin' in German. They were oaths she had learned from her husband I'm sure. But if Cleveland won she'd stick around awhile, and I'd fill her in. And we were kind of pals, even though she had seventy years on me.

That summer, one day the last part of July, she didn't pick up the paper. Next day the same. Dad was away driving truck then, and I didn't say anything about it to my mother, as she thought Mrs. Hall was a witch and, even worse, a drinker.

"She drinks *spirits,*" my mother insisted.

"No, she doesn't," I said.

"Yes, she does. I've smelled it on her."

The third day she didn't show, near dusk, I took the papers over to her house. I walked down the steps to her door and knocked. I stood there for awhile, then I just opened the door and went in.

She was laid up pretty bad. I'd never been in her house before. It ain't much to the place. One big room, with the bathroom the only thing behind a door. She don't even have electricity. She has kerosene lamps. A large oak bed that she's lying on. A kitchen table with one straightbacked chair. Many tomatoes from her garden on the sink, some of them green. Two armchairs covered with old horse blankets. A treadle sewing machine. A washboard and tub. Got many newspapers, and they're all stacked very neatly against the walls. She seemed to have saved every newspaper we had ever given her. It was cool there, damp, and smelled of must and kerosene smoke. And nearer the bed, a stale cat-like reek.

She was glad, I think, to see me. This was always hard to tell with her, as it wasn't in her to smile so much. She was thirsty, and I refilled her glass with water. I read her all the line scores for the days that had gone by. This was on a Friday. I told her the Indians hadn't played Thursday. I figured it would be alright to tell her a white lie, just this once, as they'd got their ass beat by Chicago. It wasn't even close.

But I'm not sure now that she fell for it. Or maybe that wasn't so much on her mind just then. Because she had something to tell me, and what she did say took me much of my life to comprehend.

"I ain't doin' so good," she said. "All my animals is leavin' out a me."

I barely heard her. She had a narrow nose, a hard, straight mouth. It was just as thin and straight as if drawn by pen and ruler. Her eyes were light gray. Whatever ailed her, I noticed, had left them shining unnaturally bright. It had taken the color from her face and replaced it with pallor and small red flowers on her cheeks. And the main impression of that moment which, afterwards, and now many decades past, I recall, is that I was struck just then by how she resembled a little girl there in the shadows of her bed.

"When a person starts to dyin'," she went on, "it's 'cause all their animals, they are leavin' out a them. A long time past, longer than before you were born, if I saw somebody what was dyin', an' I cared for them, I'd go to the woods an' get their animals back. . . ."

I spent all the next day in the woods across the tracks. It came a rain that day. The rain was long and sharp. But I didn't see nothing but a couple squirrels, and I couldn't figure out no way to catch them.